HEADSTRONG PRINCE

CAPTURED BY A DRAGON-SHIFTER SERIES

MICHELLE M. PILLOW

MICHELLE M. PILLOW® - MICHELLEPILLOW.COM

Headstrong Prince © Copyright 2017 - 2018 by Michelle M. Pillow

Second Printing July 2018, The Raven Books LLC

First Printing September 2017

ISBN: 978-1-62501-180-0

ABOUT HEADSTRONG PRINCE

Welcome to the dangerous world of Qurilixen where dragon-shifters and cat-shifters rule as fiercely as they love.

There is an undeniable attraction between them, but is pure chemistry enough to overcome intergalactic odds?

Prince Ivar is a cat-shifting prince from another planet, honor bound to help his people find mates. And he's determined to make this quest to Earth a success. When he crosses paths with the independent human woman, Beth Watson, he finds his world spinning on its axis.

WELCOME TO QURILIXEN

Qurilixen World Novels

Dragon Lords Series

Barbarian Prince

Perfect Prince

Dark Prince

Warrior Prince

His Highness The Duke

The Stubborn Lord

The Reluctant Lord

The Impatient Lord

The Dragon's Queen

Lords of the Var® Series
The Savage King
The Playful Prince
The Bound Prince
The Rogue Prince
The Pirate Prince

Captured by a Dragon-Shifter Series
Determined Prince
Rebellious Prince
Stranded with the Cajun
Hunted by the Dragon
Mischievous Prince
Headstrong Prince

Space Lords Series
His Frost Maiden
His Fire Maiden
His Metal Maiden
His Earth Maiden

His Woodland Maiden

Dynasty Lords Series
Seduction of the Phoenix
Temptation of the Butterfly

To learn more about the Qurilixen World series of
books and to stay up to date on the latest book list
visit www.MichellePillow.com

AUTHOR UPDATES

To stay informed about when a new book in the series installments is released, sign up for updates:

michellepillow.com/author-updates

NOTE FROM AUTHOR

IF YOU'RE new to my books, the *Dragon Lords* are my bestselling futuristic shape-shifter romance series. The stories became reader favorites, and so I wrote things from their enemy's point of view in a spin-off series for the cat-shifting *Lords of the Var*®. Then they ventured off into the stars in the series install-ment *Space Lords*. Now, I'm time traveling with them back to our time with the series *Captured by a Dragon-Shifter*, which you are now reading book one of. Don't worry, I have the series reading order on my website to help you figure it all out, http://michellepillow.com/.

To those of you *not* new to my books, readers have emailed asking Dragon Lords cultural questions since the first dragon-shifting prince released years ago. I have teased you with a lot of little hints of how the Draig found brides in "the old days". Many of you have expressed wanting to climb aboard the space ship and sail away into the future—which would probably take some cryogenic freezing and a lot of icy waiting. Well, before you start packing those sweaters... I don't want any of you going to that extreme, so I've brought your favorite dragon-shifters and cat-shifters to modern-day Earth. They don't live on our planet, but they have recently started to revisit.

For *Dragon Lords* and *Lords of the Var*® fans, *Captured by a Dragon-Shifter* is a modern-day prequel series to those first books. They take place long before the princes you know and love ever found their mates, long before *The Dragon's Queen*, in a time when the dragon-shifters and cat-shifters actually—wait for it—*liked* each other and hung out as friends. They also don't have Galaxy Brides to bring them women. There's no one left to marry on the planet and things are starting to get desperate.

AUTHOR RECOMMENDS READING series installments in order of release for the simple fact she likes hiding little tidbits in the books as she goes and it's more fun that way, though each book can be read as a standalone if you prefer.

To my new hometown.
Hotty Toddy!

1

THE SQUARE, OXFORD, MISSISSIPPI

"HOTTY TODDY!" The aggressive battle cry rang out over the plaza, a second time.

Prince Ivar of the Var immediately tensed as his urge to shift became almost insuppressible. Around him, the natives gravitated toward the man on the balcony who in turn grinned in pride at the frenzy he'd created. "Hotty Toddy!" The noise carried, echoing through the streets.

Hotty Toddy was not an exclamation Ivar had heard before. Not on his home planet of Qurilixen, at least. Actually, very little about this place reminded him of home.

Ivar's senses continued to tingle. On edge and defensive, he turned slowly, putting his back to Prince Finn of the Draig. His shifter hearing focused on the distance for any signs of trouble. He was aware of what humans thought of alien visitors from the movies he'd seen in Earth theaters. The princes were alone. There was no one to help fight off an attack. If planet officials suspected who they were, it could end badly, and they would have to make a run for the secret portal that would take them home.

The battle cry finally dissipated and nothing more happened.

"We should leave." Ivar turned his attention toward the balcony.

The commander stood next to a dining table watching them. He was not dressed as warriors on Ivar's home world, but he clearly had authority. His cheeks were flushed as if he'd been drinking, never a good thing when a man was in charge of others.

Ivar reminded himself that he had acted in error and deserved the human reprimand. He had not meant to scare the fragile human child in a pink dress as she pranced across the painted lines on the street, but the girl had tried to grab one of the cross laces holding the sides of his shirt closed. Of course he'd growled at her. She should not have touched him. He glanced back, seeing the father consoling the frightened girl.

As a cat-shifter, Ivar could either half shift or

fully shift into the form of a tiger. If he needed to disrobe quickly, he could, which is why there were cross laces along the sides of his pants and shirt. He did not wish to undress on a public human street.

"That man must be a commander." Ivar nodded toward the general on the balcony. He wore a white shirt with large blue flowers on it and short pants. He held a brown bottle in his hand and took frequent drinks from it. "See how he stands above the others surveying the area from a vantage point?"

"I don't think that was a threat," Finn corrected, clearly more curious than worried about this unexplored location. "I see no one coming for us."

Finn was Ivar's only traveling companion on this journey. When the dragon-shifter approached him with the idea to sneak onto Earth without permission from their royal parents, Ivar should have said no. He should say no now and demand they go back before anyone noticed they had left.

If anything happened, their people would not realize they were gone until it was too late and the portal, their only way home, had closed. As much as he liked Finn, Ivar knew the dragon prince was not known for being responsible. It would be up to Ivar to make sure they both made it back home safely.

"Still, perhaps we should show respect to the

local Earth authorities." Ivar turned toward the balcony, placed a fist over his heart, and then bowed, urging Finn to do the same.

The commander laughed and pointed down at them before pushing to his feet and bowing in return.

"Let us retreat to another section of this town, away from that man's sight." Ivar's words were more of a command than a suggestion. He didn't wait for Finn to answer before he started to walk.

Yes, Finn was also a prince, and their sneaking through the portal to *Miss-is-sip-pie* had been his idea, but the man was not the ideal leader for an expedition of this importance. Dragon-shifters were usually more disciplined than Finn.

Conversely, Ivar was told that he had a particular drive and discipline which was unnatural for cat-shifters. Headstrong is what his mother called it, which was a much kinder word than what Ivar's brother, Rafe, used.

Finn was too enamored with the Earth people to make wise decisions. He spoke of humans like they were simply shifters who could not shift, with a naiveté and vulnerability that made them even more fascinating to behold. Earthlings were like children in the universe, unaware of anything beyond their home. Earth was not the only planet, and humans were not the only alien race nor did they represent the only way to live. Aliens had yet to make first contact with them, and humans still lived securely in the belief that everything centered around them and their needs.

Besides, Finn rarely took anything seriously, which is why his coming to Ivar with this plan had been such a surprise. Out of all the princes, Finn never acted like he *wanted* to find a wife. Trips to Earth had been a chance to get into trouble and have adventures away from the prying eyes of their parents and the rest of shifter nobility.

This trip was different. The plan was to find wives, *any wives*, and bring the women home before anyone knew the princes were missing. If they could prove they had been well matched by the gods with human women, they could convince the assembly of elders to keep the portals open.

And that is where things became tricky. To obtain ultimate happiness, a shifter needed to find his true mate. Tonight, they were taking *any* mate. They would be married to women who were not their true mates, obligated to pretend they had found their destinies. In doing so, they would save the future of their people. The princes would be forever joined in this secret that they'd be forced to carry.

Ivar never thought Finn would have it in him to make a sacrifice that put his people before himself. If this night went as planned, Ivar's opinion of the dragon-shifter would be forever changed.

The Earth town looked familiar insomuch that it was alien constructed and appeared like the ones his people had seen on the transmission waves caught on his home world. No, Earth people called it television, not transmissions.

The structures were not like those on Ivar's planet. They were fat and square and squished together. The area centered on a large white building encircled by a road as if to mark its importance by forcing vehicles to drive around it. Across the street on all sides from the showcased building, other structures pressed tightly together with balconies above the walkway, as if to keep those humans below from looking too far past the wares and foods being sold. There was no distant landscape, no fields and forests.

When the shifters had first started coming to Earth, they tried to blend in with the locals. Ivar had told women he was a drag queen, which he quickly found out wasn't the best way to secure a bride. His people thought it meant royalty. It also turned out that Earth was diverse and had enough strange fashions and rituals that their native garb barely drew attention.

Whereas Ivar dressed like a Var, Finn wore a looser tunic style shirt over dark pants and boots common to dragon-shifters. Dragons only half shifted into what looked to be a man-dragon hybrid and did not need to strip out of their clothing. They both carried bags against their hip with thick straps across their chests. Each filled with Earth cash-money, and food rations in case they did not find anything suitable to eat.

Ivar did not want to be on Earth long. Everything about the planet made him uncomfortable. He looked around, hoping to see a woman he could take home to be his wife. It shouldn't be too hard to find a female willing to be a princess, even if it was on an alien world.

Ivar would not be the one to introduce humans to the truth of the universe. The prince simply wanted to find a mate. He would then take her through the portal to his home world to live in the Var palace, and they would never visit this primitive planet ever again.

Surely the gods would bless him this time. He did his duty. He took care of his family and his people. He'd begged them to bless him. He did everything he was supposed to do.

If the gods were with them, they'd find their true mates and be home before an hour had passed. He glanced over the crowds, suspiciously watching the locals. The swish of a white skirt caught his attention as a woman disappeared around a corner. He had the urge to follow her but stopped himself.

Who was he kidding? He wasn't sure the will of the gods could be heard in a place full of so much noise and clutter.

There were no women appropriate for mating that he could see. He'd thought the shifter scouts had marked this location as unusable because of the semi-public location of the portal opening when it materialized. In fact, it might have been because every female he could see was either too young or appeared to be wearing a marriage finger shackle.

Ivar thought of his younger brother. Rafe's wife, Jenna, came from Earth and the two of them had a stable union. They'd met in a place where humans procured food. If his brother's happiness were any indication, such a meeting place would be lucky.

Finn's brother had found his wife in a tavern. Eve had been on a stage singing bizarre words. She'd also been drunk. Ivar would never question the will of the gods, and they chose Eve to be a princess, but he had come to the conclusion that most tavern women were not looking for mates. Ivar liked Eve well enough but did not want such a handful for his bride.

"You're quieter than usual," Finn said, as they moved down the sidewalk away from the town center. The further they walked, the fewer people they saw. Buildings turned into large houses that were set back from the street. "Are you having second thoughts about our mission?"

"No," Ivar said without hesitation. "I was thinking that I do not understand why those dragons would choose to defect through the portal to live here permanently."

Ivar instantly wished he wouldn't have broached the subject.

Finn frowned. "One problem at a time. If we keep the portals open, I plan to find the lost dragons and bring them home. I think I have narrowed down which location they have been using. It is a place called New Orleans. I honestly believe the only reason they left our world was to find brides. I cannot blame them for that. By going through with our plan to prove happiness in marriage is possible, and to regulate travel, we can end future defection."

"New Orleans? I am not sure I have been to that portal stop," Ivar said.

"My brother has been there with his wife. When Eve was kidnapped by a cat-shifter from the Nutef faction and brought there to die, Kyran went after her. I have traced the time when the dragon-shifters left, and it seems to point to that location. We have extra guards assigned to prevent future problems. If I can get them to come home, it will calm many of the fears and rumors about Earth."

Ivar didn't speak.

"I know this was my idea, and I'll understand if *you* change *your* mind," Finn said.

"I will not change my mind." Ivar again did not hesitate. He knew what needed to be done. "I don't like the idea of taking women against their will, but I have not changed my mind."

"Kidnapped brides are not what either of us wants, and I pray it will never come to that. I keep asking myself, what if the women don't want to be married, or if they make us miserable? What if they are unkind or driven by vanity and ego?"

As much as he didn't like Finn's impetuous attitude, seeing him worried was almost worse. "Then we will have to smile, and lie, and pretend to love our wives for the rest of our hundreds of years. We agreed, and I do not wish to change my course. You were right. This is the only way to force the elders to keep the portals open. Without brides, our people die out. This will be the secret we carry to our graves. It is a sacrifice we must be willing to make."

"I don't think Lord Montague will ever be convinced to keep the portals open," Finn said. Lord Montague was not only a dragon elder but also the stoic leader of the dragon council of elders. He was the most outspoken when it came to closing portal travel forever.

"If you convince the other elders, then there's nothing he can do to stop it." Ivar had never seen Lord Montague with anything but a look of disapproval and disgust on his face. He doubted the man liked anything.

They had snuck through the portal for a reason and could not lose sight of that goal. Tonight was not about love. The odds of the gods blessing them were not great. They'd tried so many times before with no luck. Yes, they hoped to find their true mates, but if that didn't happen—one way or another—they would be leaving with women.

The plan was to defy tradition and create their own blessing. They would take half mates, ensure the future of the shifter population, and never let a moment of discontentment show.

Cat-shifters had taken half mates in the past, but those were marriages of convenience. Ivar wanted a love like his parents had, like his brother had, but this wasn't about his wants. He was a prince. He had a duty to his people as did Finn. What mattered more? The fates of two princes? Or the survival of thousands?

"I keep hoping women will walk up to us and say, 'The gods sent us to you. We are your true mates. Take us home and prove to the elders that human women make viable wives and the portal should be left open so that others may come and be happy.' But I know that is unlikely," Finn said.

"If only it were that easy." Ivar agreed the fantasy had appeal, but he did not want to be drawn into fanciful daydreams. "We should not place our bets on such horrible odds."

A young man walked past them and gave them a strange look.

"We should use the Earth language." Ivar hadn't realized they'd slipped into their native tongue. They initially had learned to speak the Earth languages from the television transmission waves floating around space and then furthered their vocabulary as those first scouts came to investigate the portal openings.

"Like our talking about the decreasing population of dragon-shifters and cat-shifters due to a lack of females would draw less attention than our foreign words." Finn laughed. "Maybe we should announce ourselves. Perhaps the women would line up to marry us."

"I'm glad you find amusement in this." Ivar's tone expressed the opposite. He wasn't glad. Not about any of this. He couldn't help the sternness in his voice. The future of his people was not a game.

"I'm sorry, Ivar. I do not mean to make light. I know you do not want to be on this planet. You have made that clear on every trip to Earth we have taken." Finn took a deep breath. "I don't want to do this either. I want a wife, but not like this."

"There is nothing down this road but houses and traffic," Finn said. "We should turn around."

"Agreed. We do not want to wander too far from the portal." Ivar followed Finn's lead, and they moved in the other direction. "We will stay close to that central location where there are many gathering places and hope that more women appear."

They quickened their pace to hurry back toward the center of town. Turning down a small inlet with tables, they heard people talking. Children screamed, running with their hands in the air as they carried colorful ice cream cones.

Ivar lifted his hands wide to the side. "I did nothing this time to make them scream. I didn't even look at them."

"I think that sound is excitement, not fear," Finn said.

"You have to come back here for a football game this fall," a boisterous voice demanded. They turned to watch the commander from the balcony pass by the inlet. "We might not win all the games, but we never lose a party. The fun starts at the tailgating and doesn't end until dawn."

"I think ol' Donald here secretly works for the tourist board," one of the commander's men teased. The group walked on, and Ivar let go of his captured breath. He did not want to be blamed for frightening more children.

"What is football?" Finn asked.

Ivar gestured that he did not know.

"Perhaps we will have better luck if we take different paths," Finn suggested. "We do not have much time, and we can cover more ground apart."

Ivar nodded. "The sound does carry here. Stay within shouting distance to the center. If that portal closes, we're trapped for a year until it reopens. We both need to be gone before that happens."

Finn's expression turned unusually serious as he looked around. "No. Of course we wouldn't want that."

"The commander has left." For some reason, Ivar was drawn to where he'd seen the woman in the white skirt. Perhaps if he followed in that direction, there would be more women. "I'll head back the way we came. You can explore here. If either of us finds suitable brides, we will meet in the middle."

"A fine plan," Finn agreed.

Before the man could leave Ivar placed a hand on his arm to stop him. He wanted to say something comforting, but there were no words. "We have to believe that kindness in a mate will be enough and that happiness can be found in duty."

Finn didn't answer.

Ivar had seen the look on his brother's face each time Jenna entered the room. He saw their love, their devotion, and their contentment. As pleased as he was for Rafe, their happiness over the last few years had made Ivar's loneliness worse.

"We will not have that mad rush of passion that others talk about," Ivar continued, "but in the end, our pleasure will have to come from seeing others find mates. If that is the sacrifice the gods demand, then we will pay it."

"Yes. We will pay it." Finn nodded sadly.

Before Ivar could say anything more, Finn took off through the inlet in the same direction the children had come from.

Ivar wondered if the dragon prince was reconsidering their decision. He couldn't say it would surprise him. When the time came to decide, he wasn't sure how Finn would act.

2

"Y'ALL, some guy just asked me to marry him."

Beth Watson glanced up from the viewing screen on her camera to look at the college-age girl who spoke to her friends. The girl had brunette hair that fell nearly to her waist and shorts that had been cut a little too high.

"Who?" the boy with her asked. He puffed up his chest as if he'd do something about it. He was also a college student if his fraternity t-shirt and cargo shorts were any indications. Beth would have guessed him to be a freshman or sophomore at her alma mater.

The girl laughed, enthusiastically leading her friends. "Some guy."

"I don't think he was talking to you, Jenny," a

woman with short blonde hair put forth. Her shirt read, "Stacy," and she sounded like she came from Louisiana. Her wry tone deflated some of her friend's ego. "I think he was talking to the waitress."

"But she was old," Jenny protested.

"Yeah," Stacy said. "And so was the guy."

"Whatever. Let's get ice cream," Jenny quickly changed directions, forcing the others to do the same.

It had only been six years since Beth had been roaming these very streets in groups like that, but what a difference those six years made.

She had come back to Oxford to visit a couple of her favorite professors. And if the truth were told, ask for career advice and perhaps a boost of encouragement. The real world was hard and trying to make a go with her art was even more challenging. There were times she thought about stopping altogether and trying her hand at teaching, or some full-time office job. But at the end of the day, she still picked up her camera and paintbrushes.

The kids' banter reminded her of simpler times when she first moved to Mississippi to attend college from upstate New York. It had been a culture shock. Strangers had talked to her and shown her kindness, and their laid back approach to life wasn't anything she'd experienced growing up. Not that any place was perfect, but even the insults in the South sounded polite. People waved, and she had a neighbor bring her a welcome gift when she moved into her first off campus apartment. It was this feeling of positivity she wanted to capture on film and translate into her paintings.

After college, Beth had moved to New Orleans with the idea that she would soak in the creative atmosphere to fuel her art. What she'd discovered was that the city had plenty of artists doing the exact same thing and if she wanted to feel original, she had to leave New Orleans for places like Oxford to gain inspiration. She could then return home, using the creative energy to realize those visions.

"Lovely evening, isn't it?"

Beth turned her attention from the settings on her camera to the friendly voice. The man was handsome, with kind dark eyes and a playful smile. She nodded before turning back to her camera. "Yes, it is."

"I see you are not shackled."

At that, Beth turned her full attention to the man. He wore a hippie kind of outfit that looked more like loose pajamas, or the lightweight white beach pants guys sometimes wore when walking next to the ocean. His words had an unfamiliar accent, but the college hosted international professors, so that wasn't necessarily unusual.

"Shackled?" she asked.

He held up his hand and pointed at the ring finger. "Married."

"Oh," Beth gave a small laugh. "I'd never heard it put quite like that before. Yes, actually, I am married. My ring is being cleaned."

A lie was nicer than shooting the man's forthcoming offer down.

"I see." His expression fell. "Would you happen to know women who are not married?"

"You might try the bar just down there." She gestured down the street where a couple of bars could be found. "And, uh, I'm sorry, I didn't catch your name."

"Finn."

Beth smiled, wondering if this was the same guy Jenny had been talking about. "Finn, my advice would be to start with asking for a date instead of a wedding. You're more likely to get a yes."

The man nodded and moved in the direction she indicated. Beth found something about his expression to be charming, but she wasn't in the market for a complication. She needed to focus on her work.

With purpose, she set about making the most of

her trip. She lifted her camera and focused on happy couples like a voyeur peeking into the window of other people's lives. Ok, so maybe that analogy wasn't exactly right. She wasn't invading privacy on a public street, but she was capturing moments.

Seeing a cheerful couple, she sighed. They looked a little too perfect, like actors on a movie casting call, and she lowered the camera. Normally she was fine being single, but there were small moments when a longing struck her, and she wanted what other people had. What person wouldn't want that kind of perfect, happily ever after love?

Beth didn't dwell long. She lifted the camera with renewed determination, intent on finding her vision for the next collection.

3

"Divide and conquer," Ivar muttered to himself, without knowing the true meaning of the words as he hurried off in the opposite direction. He'd heard the phrase in a movie, like everything else he knew about Earth.

He and Finn had divided to cover more territory, but Ivar wasn't doing much conquering. He'd tried to follow down the same path the woman in white had gone earlier, but it only led him to a parking lot. Hopefully, Finn was having more luck.

As the hours stretched, Ivar knew they didn't have much time before the portal closed. "I found two," Finn said, clearly excited as he jogged to catch up to where Ivar stood. "They're waiting for us at the portal."

"What?" Ivar asked in surprise. He began walking toward the portal, hoping to catch a glimpse of them. His heartbeat quickened. "Where?"

"They're of the right age. They're pretty. They appear kind," Finn said, walking at a fast pace. "They are perhaps a bit too delicate, but—"

"All Earth women are fragile," Ivar dismissed. Kind was good. He wanted a princess who was kind to the people. "That is to be expected."

"The hour turns late." Finn rushed ahead toward the passageway labeled, "Faulkner Alley," and said, "They are waiting near the portal for us."

"I don't understand." Ivar hurried to keep up. They had a few moments before the portal closed. Finn was clearly eager if his urgency was any indication. "How did you convince them to come?"

Finn paused before crossing the street and grinned. He made a sweeping gesture with his hand to encompass his full length. "What woman can resist the smooth charm of a dragon?"

Ivar fought the urge to respond to the grandiose claim. They didn't stop as they crossed the circular street toward the central white building before crossing a second time to reach the shadowed passageway. His eyes shifted to better see into the dim light. The passage was empty. Luckily, the locals appeared to keep to the lit streets. Ivar glanced over the immediate area for the women Finn spoke of but saw no one who seemed to be waiting for them. He moved through the passageway to the other side. Again, no women were waiting.

Ivar moved toward the black door with the metal skull hanging from it in the middle of the passage. His senses tingled as a suspicious feeling came over him. "Where are the women? You said you found them for us."

"They were excited. I bet they already found their way through." Finn motioned that Ivar should go into the portal. They used the door as a landmark since it was right next to where the portal manifested. "Just beyond the black door. You should go in after them. The caves will be dark on the other side of the portal, and they might be frightened."

The women should not have gone through alone. Ivar frowned as he moved toward the black door. He made sure no one watched him as he lifted his hand. The tips of his fingers grazed the brick wall, activating a soft light for the barest of seconds. He couldn't shake the feeling that something was wrong.

"Hey, are you guys in line for that secret grilled cheese place?" A young man called down the alley.

Ivar jerked his hand back, to keep the portal from being seen. "I don't think you can get in this early."

"No," Ivar and Finn answered loudly in unison.

"Oh, doesn't look like you're dressed for it, anyway." He left.

"This place is odd." Ivar lowered his hand and didn't go through. He trusted his instincts and right now they said Finn was hiding something. The dragon-shifter was acting strange, and it made no sense that he would let the women out of his sight. Ivar narrowed his eyes and motioned that Finn should go. "You first."

"What?" Finn gave a dismissing laugh. "Go ahead. I'm right behind you."

Ivar crossed his arms over his chest. "I insist."

"It will close soon." Finn tried to give Ivar a small push. "Stop playing around and go."

Ivar barely registered the man's shove. At that moment, he read everything he needed to know in Finn's gaze. "There are no women, are there?"

Finn looked guilty. "No. You're right. There are not. I had hoped that fate would smile on us, and we'd find the ones we were meant to be with, but I wasn't forthcoming about the plan in coming here." He again tried to get Ivar to go through.

Ivar held his ground. He was disappointed that

the mission had been a failure, but did not know why Finn felt the need to lie about it. The hour was getting late, and they needed to go home. If both princes did not return, chaos would erupt on the planet. If only one prince returned and people found out the other was left behind, it could be war. "Get in the portal. We will discuss this on our home world."

Finn shook his head. "I'm not going back. I'm staying for the next year. I need you to tell our parents they can't cave in the portals. I am a prince. They will not leave me behind. This is the only way to negotiate more time for our people. You know as well as I what the elders are going to demand at that meeting. They have been seeking an excuse to cut off Earth since the directions to the portal were first unearthed in the Draig royal library. They are scared of things that are no longer threats."

Ivar couldn't believe what he was hearing. Was Finn insane? Taking unfated brides was one thing, but choosing to live on Earth like the other defectors? There was no way he was abandoning Finn to this planet. He started to protest the foolishness of the plan when Finn cut him off.

"Look at this world, Ivar. There are no more shifter hunters. There are no more knights. There aren't even the castles the old ones talk about. We don't exist in this world but in fairy tales and fantasy. Convince them that this is for the best for both cats and dragons. When the portal to this place opens back up, I will be here, waiting."

This was insanity. Finn was a prince. He could not stay alone on Earth for a year.

"I'm not leaving you behind." Ivar frowned, ready to throw Finn through to the other side if he had to. "How will you survive on this planet? I am looking around, and they are a primitive, strange people. They do not even acknowledge the existence of beings beyond their skies. How vain are these humans to think they are the only ones to crawl out of the infinite?"

"Your feelings are exactly why I didn't tell you my intentions. I had hoped it wouldn't come to this, but the gods are not smiling upon us."

His intentions? This had been Finn's plan all along? To trick him back through the portal if they didn't find women, and to stay behind? What would Ivar say to the Draig queen and king? It would look like he abandoned the dragon prince.

"We don't have time to debate." Finn held open the satchel he carried. The evening light cast them into shadows, but the artificial lights illuminated just enough of the alleyway that someone might see them arguing. "I assure you I have thought this through. I will be fine. I brought supplies. I have Earth cash-money papers, dried meat, clothes—"

"Unacceptable," Ivar broke in. "I forbid you from staying."

"You have no authority over me. You can't forbid me from doing anything. This isn't Var territory."

"And you're not a prince here, dragon," Ivar insisted. Did the man not realize the stupidity of what he was proposing? "You have no protection, no way of calling for help."

"Nobility does not change with location," Finn argued.

"Your royalty is not recognized here." Ivar snatched the satchel of supplies from Finn, and demanded, "Get in the portal, or I will throw you in. I will not leave you."

"I left a note explaining this to the king and queen, in my room at the palace. Now, go and be well. I'll be here in a year," Finn promised. He grabbed his supplies back.

There was clearly no reasoning with him. Ivar surged forward and took hold of the dragon prince, grabbing him by his shirtfront.

"You're going home," Ivar commanded, trying to

drag him to the opening. Finn's shirt ripped in their struggle. "Get in the portal."

"No." Finn swept his hand to get free as Ivar strengthened his hold.

"Get in the portal." This time Ivar punched. He was done playing around.

"No." Finn made a sound of defiance and ducked before Ivar's fist could make contact. He pushed at Ivar's waist, trying to force him through.

Ivar resisted, spinning Finn around. The man bounced close to the opening, but brick stopped him from going anywhere.

Finn charged, trying to knock the bigger man off his footing. It didn't work. His attempts only annoyed Ivar.

A shift threatened to ripple over Ivar's flesh, but he didn't care. Claws grew from the tips of his fingers. Finn needed to get into that portal and Ivar was going to make sure the prince made it home—conscious or not. They could spar it out on their home world later.

Finn tried to growl in warning, but Ivar wasn't scared of dragons.

"Get in the portal, Finn," Ivar said, louder than before.

Finn punched. Ivar let the man land the blow

against his jaw. A jolt of pain worked its way over his face as he absorbed the attack, but the fact he didn't dodge made Finn lose his footing.

"Stop, or I'll call the cops!" The feminine cry distracted Finn long enough for Ivar to gain the advantage. A bright light moved toward them. The woman approached holding up a rectangular Earth communication device.

Ivar didn't hesitate. He punched, knocking Finn senseless. The man could be angry with him later. But Finn was going home.

Ivar tossed him at the brick wall. Finn disappeared inside the portal with a flash of purple light. The woman screamed.

Ivar turned his attention to her. She stood, eyes wide in fear as she stared at him. It was then he realized that he was half shifted, and she'd just witnessed portal travel. Fangs protruded from his elongated mouth, and tiger fur covered his face and hands. His vision was sharp, and he knew his eyes would be glowing in the darkness from the power of the shift.

Sacred cats!

This wasn't good. He couldn't leave a witness behind.

Ivar held up his hands in an effort to keep her calm, but she screamed and tried to run. He panicked and gave chase. It wasn't hard to catch her. She moved like a human and was no match for his speed and agility.

He covered her mouth to keep her from making more noise and drawing attention. Humans were so delicate, and he had no desire to hurt her. Yet he couldn't let the humans find the way to his home planet.

She kicked her legs, and he regretted her fear. The gateway would be closing soon, and he needed to make a decision.

"I'm sorry," he whispered, hoping she could register his apology and forgive him for what he had to do, "but this secret can't be revealed."

Ivar pushed her into the portal after Finn. He'd have to make it up to her on the other side. Once they explained and made her understand, they could return her. Or, perhaps this was the gods telling him to take the woman home. He did not feel like she was meant to be his mate, but then he wasn't looking for a true mate. She could be his princess, and he could fulfill part of their plan to save the future of the shifters.

Ivar waited a few seconds to give her time to pass through before jumping after her. He was ready to get off this floating rock. It was time to go home.

He closed his eyes and held his breath, waiting for the sensation of portal travel, that painful moment when everything collapsed in on him, and he couldn't breathe. Sound would become a deafening roar. Instead, sharp pain radiated down his arm as he crashed into a hard surface.

Ivar opened his eyes to see he was still in the alleyway. This time he watched as he jumped toward the place Finn and the woman had disappeared into. He again slammed into the wall. He tried a third time, and a fourth, then a fifth and sixth, beating himself against the brick wall in desperation. When that didn't work, he struck his hands against the stone.

Nothing.

He hit the brick harder, trying to break through. All traces of the portal light were gone, leaving him in shadows. Blood smeared the white paint covering the brick. He breathed harder, desperation turning to despair. His forearm bled from where he'd scraped it, blood dripping onto the ground at his feet. He ignored the pain.

No. Not this. Anything but this.

He couldn't be trapped on Earth. Alone.

Not this.

Not this.

His hand pressed into the hard surface until the rectangle shape was embedded into his skin. For a long moment, he mentally willed his hand to fall through, to give him a safe journey home.

"Finn?" he whispered as if his friend could hear him and somehow reopen the portal to let him pass. Unfortunately, that was not how the Qurilixian portal worked. It would only open to this location once every Earth year, and only for a short period of time, and only if someone from the other side activated it first. He had no choice but to find another portal opening on this alien world, or wait a year.

A year on Earth.

Alone.

Ivar could only remember a handful of times when he felt real fear. First, as he watched a spaceship land like a giant fiery saucer from the sky and he met his first alien visitor as a boy. The day the scientists announced there was nothing they could do to help the cat-shifter population reproduce more female children. When his brother's wife had been kidnaped by the Nutef faction, and they'd almost lost her. And this moment right here.

Ivar did not know his way around Earth. When the shifters visited, it was only for a few hours, and they always left the way they came. He looked up, unable to see the sky from his place within the narrow corridor between buildings. How was he supposed to find a location when the stars here made no sense? On Qurilixen he could track anyone or anything. He read the natural signs in the shadowed marshes and in the forests as clearly as if he looked at a map. No matter where he was on his home world, he could find the Var palace.

"Finn," he said again, knowing it was pointless.

His heart hammered violently. Adrenaline pumped through his veins, a residual effect from having thrown Prince Finn—and the woman who had the misfortune of coming through the alley during their argument—through the portal. His knuckles stung from where he'd punched the man. Ivar should have known that Finn was up to something when the mischievous dragon-shifter invited him on a secret trip to Earth.

"Stupid dragon, what were you thinking? You knew I would not allow you to stay here alone. You should have just gone through the portal, instead of making me throw you through. We would have figured out a better way to convince the elders to keep the path open."

The metal skull on the black door next to the portal entrance seemed to mock him. Ivar should have heeded the warning the second he saw it. The gods had been telling him to turn around. He dared to defy them by planning to take a bride before they deemed him worthy. This was his punishment.

Earth was strange, and the Earthlings who inhabited it even stranger. Ivar wanted to go home. He couldn't be trapped here.

Ivar slammed his hand against the wall. His claws chipped at the line of mortar between bricks. In his heightened state, he had forgotten he was partially shifted. A half cat, half man would surely send a panic through the city, and with no escape, he could imagine what kind of welcome the locals would give him. He'd heard stories from the elders. He'd seen the films.

"Whoa," a young human male called out in surprise, looking down the corridor at him. "Dude, check this out." He waved, and another young man appeared next to him. Lifting his voice, the first man said to Ivar, "Hey, are you like doing a movie or something? Cool costume."

A small growl left Ivar's throat instead of Earth words. The noise only seemed to delight the humans, and they began laughing and telling each other how "freaking cool" the "dude" was.

Ivar touched his fur-covered arm. Heat radiated

from his skin. He was not cool. In fact, he was quite the opposite.

Ivar pulled into the shadows, thankful that the planet had darkened. He shifted to human form before coming out of the corridor onto the street. He rushed down the sidewalk so the bizarre dude-humans couldn't follow him.

The satchel he carried only had a little food and cash-money. It wasn't enough to last him an entire year. Back home, he might be a prince, but here he was nobody. No one would know who he was, or be compelled to help him. Ivar would have to fend for himself. He'd have to forage for strange foods and hope they were not poisonous. He needed to find shelter nearby to stay close to the portal.

The crowd had thickened with the evening hours, and they flowed past him like water around a stone. Their Earth words were a jumbled sea of white noise, and even though he could speak the language, he was having a hard time understanding them.

Where should he go? What should he do? He did not want to be here. His thoughts traveled too fast. He needed to apply reasoning and come up with a plan of action.

Ivar found himself walking with the crowd,

unsure where he'd end up. He wanted to go home. How could he get home?

For a brief moment, he paused and closed his eyes. The sound did not stop. The air did not change. Movement continued all around him.

As he made his way along the sidewalk, he found himself in an open courtyard. A metal statue had been mounted on a bench, forever posed as if ready for conversation. Ivar ducked off the main path, out of the crowd, and sat down beside the statue. He didn't move as he studied the Earthlings. It was hard to believe this planet had once been home to cat-shifters. There was nothing familiar about it, no castles, and no ceffyls grazing in a field.

He was unsure how much time passed. The crowds surged and then lessened. A white skirt caught his attention. He held his breath as a woman moved past. It was the same skirt he'd seen when they first arrived. His eyes swept upward, along her body. The streetlights revealed the shadowed shape of her legs beneath the material. It was enough to tease but not be inappropriate. She stopped to talk to someone on the sidewalk. Full lips parted slightly as light brown eyes glanced in his direction. She reached into a bag she carried and pulled out a peculiar device.

The predator within him surged, wanting to claw its way out. Is that what the device did? Made him reveal his true self? There was still so much he didn't know about Earth.

Ivar forgot his troubles as he watched her. She entranced him like a powerful *gullveig*. It became apparent at that moment humans had not lost their supernatural roots. How else did he explain the spell this woman cast on him with her magical device?

He fought the shift, forcing the wild beast back down. But, keeping the physical transformation at bay did nothing to stop the need he felt to go to her. He pushed up from the bench. He used his enhanced sight and hearing to focus in on her from across the distance.

The woman took a step back, bumping into a man in a white suit passing behind her. The man had a long, white mustache that stood out from the facial hair of other humans. If he spoke, the words didn't register for Ivar who was concentrating on one thing —getting to the female.

"Excuse me." She didn't talk to Ivar, didn't even appear to see his approach, but that didn't matter. Her voice was soft, and it called to him like a comforting song. He had to get to her.

Ivar moved to follow her, enthralled to hear

more. This woman in white sent him a wave of hope in an otherwise bleak world. He had to talk to her, to touch her, to...

"Pardon me, ma'am," the man answered, lifting a hat from his head as he stepped aside. He blocked the woman from Ivar's view and cut off the stream of the prince's frantic thoughts. Ivar stopped, realizing what he was in the process of doing. He had been on the verge of grabbing the woman and dragging her to...

To where? He had nowhere to go. Nothing to offer a woman.

When the mustached man stepped aside, Ivar expected to see her. His heart beat as if he'd just run the entire length of the shadowed marshes. But she had disappeared. There was no trace of her within the groups milling about.

That didn't stop the prince from trying to find her. He scanned the street for a white skirt and silky brown hair. He rushed down the walkway, wanting just one more glimpse.

She was gone.

For that single instant, he'd forgotten where he was. When he had looked at her, everything that happened made sense. However, the moment was fleeting and could not last as reality once again intruded.

What would he have done if he caught up to her? What life could he have offered her? He had nothing, not even his name or title, to trade upon. He had tried to betray the gods by attempting to take matters into his own hands, and this was how he was to be punished. The woman in white was a sign, a reminder that he had no control over what the gods chose to bless him with.

He returned to the bench next to the statue and watched across the street, hoping for a purple light to show him the way home. The only other option was to hunt down the missing dragon-shifters in the place Finn called New Orleans. Perhaps they could help him? Maybe together they could all go home?

Ivar frowned. He was a cat-shifting prince. He would be the last person defected dragon-shifters would want to show up, learning their secrets to survival—if they had even survived. No one knew for sure.

He felt even more alone.

4

BETH RUBBED her arm where the man bumped her and made her way back to her car in the free parking lot. She had to wait as a group of college kids blocked her way down the stairs leading behind the shops. She instantly recognized Jenny and Stacy and the two boys that had been following them earlier.

"I'm telling you, we saw a cat-man," the frat boy said with obvious enthusiasm.

"Ok, so show us. Where's the proof?" Jenny demanded.

"He got away before we could take a video of him," the boy explained. "Tell them, Joe."

"Clint's right," the second boy, apparently named Joe, answered. "He has to be here somewhere. This guy had tiger fur everywhere. Like a fuzzy shape-shifter man-cat."

"Exactly, a shape-shifter," Clint exclaimed.

"Cat-man? You two have been watching way too many superhero movies," Jenny dismissed.

"You like cats, Jenn, you'd probably want to take him home as a pet," Clint teased.

"Probably. Was he cute?" Jenny countered.

"I'll let you pet me." Joe pulled down his neckline to show his somewhat hairy chest.

Jenny reached over and plucked out one of his hairs.

"Ouch!" Joe swatted at her hand.

"My aunt told me that lizard men were living down in the bayou," Stacy offered.

"I heard about that urban legend on the internet." Jenny nodded. "They debunked it. Some hotel in the swamps made it up to draw tourists."

"No, it's true. My aunt's neighbor, Ursa, told her that they like to wrestle with gators in the swamp," Stacy said. "And they skinny dip in the water. So if you're lucky you can see a sexy naked man—"

"No," Joe and Clint said in unison, pretending to be dramatic.

"We don't want to hear about naked lizard men wrestling alligators," Joe said.

"Alligator Man isn't real. Cat-man is," Clint insisted.

"Excuse me," Beth politely tried to inch past the group when it became evident they weren't in a hurry to move out of the way. As much as she'd like to hear about the mythical cat-man legend these kids were trying to spin, she needed sleep.

They all glanced at her and finally began to move toward the parking lot. Beth watched them walk away as Jenny started complaining about not wanting to share a bathroom with her three roommates during the upcoming school year.

Beth had to get up early to drive home in the morning. She could expect to be on the road for a little over five hours if she pushed through with minimal stops. It would be just in time to report to work for a double shift at the restaurant she waitressed at. It wasn't glamorous, but the tips on the weekends were decent during the summer—not as good as Mardi Gras season but decent—and she needed the cash.

"Tomorrow is just another day," she told herself, getting into her car as she mentally planned her schedule. "A little sleep, then I'll be home before I know it, work, and then finally sleep again. It'll be a long one, but I can do this."

5

NEW ORLEANS, APPROXIMATELY ELEVEN
MONTHS LATER...

"IT'S GOOD, but it doesn't tell me who *you* are. I want to know *you*, Beth. I don't want to see cute. I want to see your essence. What is in your soul?" Maura said.

Beth chipped at the yellow trapped in her cuticles. Paint always seemed to hide somewhere on her person. Such was the life of an artist. She'd showered and put on her lucky white skirt and blue top, though it didn't appear to be bringing her much luck during this meeting.

The so-called professional continued to examine Beth's paintings, commenting on her lack of depth, the unrealized potential of her voice, the inauthenticity of her style. If anyone else had been listening to this conversation, Beth couldn't imagine what they would have thought. Maura Masters used big words —big hurtful words—with the ease of someone ordering their favorite dessert off a menu. The only thing she did like was the way Beth signed her name, "Bethany Watson," in the corner. Apparently, it was ideally located and of a good size.

It is one opinion, Beth told herself. *One person's opinion. They're allowed their opinion.*

Maura clearly did not like Beth's work.

The industrial-style shared office space had allowed her to display her art in the front lounge for this meeting. Concrete floors and exposed brick-and-mortar walls gave the area an artist-friendly vibe. She was glad she'd only seen one person walking to a back office so her embarrassment wouldn't be overheard.

Maura came from a New York gallery and had agreed to look at Beth's paintings. If she'd liked them, this would have been a huge break in Beth's career. Beth had so much nervousness and hope when she woke up that morning. Now the nerves were gone, and that hope was crushed under Maura's expensive heels.

Beth knew she needed to be grateful for this opportunity, and grateful for the time Maura was taking to talk to her. That didn't mean the words were easy to hear. She'd worked so hard on the current collection, planning and painting non-stop for eleven months. Despite what Maura thought, Beth had been inspired by the deep green of Mississippi's landscapes, by the blue of the summer skies, by the smiles of strangers, and the influx of excited college students who descended on the city of Oxford each August to start classes. She tried to capture the spirit of the South, not the controversy.

"It needs to be," Maura tilted her head and tapped her finger on her chin, "edgier."

As an artist, Beth knew that interpretation of a vision was influenced by who the person was, the jadedness of their upbringing, the way they interacted with and saw the world, the experiences they've had. People clearly didn't want to see happy things—at least not people like Maura whose opinion mattered in the art world. Beth tried to see things the way others saw them. Maybe that was her problem. She had no real opinion of her own. Her vision was too convoluted by the outside, by seeing others how they saw themselves but forming no solid conclusions.

Empathy?

No, that wasn't the right word.

Understanding? Sympathy? Compassion? Not, quite. It would come to her. Maybe—

"Beth?" Maura eyed her with a small frown.

"I was considering your words," Beth lied. In truth, she'd drowned out the woman's negativity and only half listened.

"You were considering whether or not I could look at the photography collection?" Maura asked.

Had the woman requested to see her photos? Beth had completely missed the question.

"Yes, of course," Beth turned and pulled out her portfolio. She laid it on the table. Occasionally, she'd sell a photograph, but typically she used them as references for her paintings.

"Hmm," Maura said to herself, as she flipped the pages. When she'd gone through half the book, she said, "You're close. Not there, but close. It's hard to explain. The technique is well thought out."

Close?

Maura joined her hands and lifted them to her mouth in thought. "A muse. That's what you need. Something or someone that stirs your insides and makes you feel when you look at it. Something that makes you so desperate to paint that you'd use your own blood if you had to."

Beth turned to her paintings, wanting to defend

her work. She couldn't help some of the doubts that surfaced. Maura Masters was distinguished. She'd be a fool not to listen to what the woman had to say.

Maura flipped through a few more pages and stopped at one Beth had taken months before. It had been an accident—one she hadn't even known was on her camera until she'd returned home. Someone had bumped into her on the street, and her lens had moved. What it captured had haunted Beth's dreams.

A handsome man appeared as if he was reaching across the distance. Surely, it was some distortion of light, but his eyes glowed with green. Intensity radiated off him. Part of his leg was blurred, captured in movement by the dim streetlights. His face was distorted as if patches of orange somehow marred his features like a bizarre, supernatural birthmark.

Beth had no idea how she'd not seen him that night visiting downtown Oxford. The man's clothes looked like something from an underground club in New York, not the shorts with athletic t-shirts or lightweight dress shirts she was used to seeing there. Laces threaded down the sides of his pants, pulled tight as if it was the only thing holding them together. The tank top also had laces down the sides. Peeks of skin showed through the thin straps.

"I forgot that was in there," Beth said apologetically as Maura continued to stare at it. The man's face had become an obsession of sorts, conjured by her dreams, and demanding attention in raw, fevered paintings she would probably never show anyone.

"It's your best work," Maura said. "It shows me your potential. Do you have more from this shoot?"

"No, I don't," Beth said as she shook her head. She wasn't sure how she felt about her "best work" being the product of an accident but said nothing. The man had been a face in a crowd that she missed but that her camera had accidentally found. She hadn't met him, didn't know his name, would most likely never see him again as he was a tourist in another state. She also couldn't get him out of her head.

"It's time to decide a path." Maura grabbed Beth's shoulders and held tight. Her metal bracelets jingled. She looked deeply into Beth's eyes as if that somehow added to the seriousness of her words. "You can keep doing what you're doing, and sell your work to banks and doctor's offices, perhaps illustrate a few children's books, and probably make a very decent living doing it. There is nothing wrong with not chasing the art gallery dream. Or you can step out of your shell and get knocked around a few times. The elite artists are nothing without their passion and pain. You need heartache. People want to see your agony poured onto the canvas. They want your metaphorical blood. You need to be crushed and come up swinging. You need to take risks. Tap into your deep subconscious and expose its vulnerabilities. What are your ecstasies? What are your fears?"

Maura took a deep breath and let Beth go. Beth couldn't move. She looked at her paintings, trying to see them for the bland emotional expression Maura saw.

"Find your passion," Maura pointed at the man's photo. "Find *that* moment again. Then bring those next samples to Ron. If he thinks you're ready, have him email me pictures from your next collection." Maura tossed a business card down on top of Beth's portfolio and left.

Beth kept the card in her photography portfolio and zipped it closed. She thought about taking her paintings down but then decided if they were meant to grace the walls of an office, they were right where they needed to be.

She lived close to the French Quarter, so it was only a short drive to her apartment from the shared office space. Her phone rang, but she ignored it. It was only her neighbor Yvonne wanting to remind her she was coming home the following day. The woman would leave a message and Beth would text her later. After such a harsh critique, Beth wanted to crawl into bed and hide.

Starting over was never easy, but it was part of the process. Maura's was one opinion. There would be others. She couldn't lose heart.

"Edgier," Beth whispered, trying to pick apart the criticisms to find what she could use going forward. "Passion? Take more chances."

It was true Beth had never had her heart broken. She'd thought she had once when she was a dramatic teenager in love with the idea of being in love. As she sat crying on her best friend's living room floor, lamenting her breakup with... *Gah*, what was his name? Troy. Yes, Troy. As she sat lamenting her breakup with Troy, the truth had hit her with such clarity. She cried because she felt she needed to, because that is what the other girls did, not because she actually ached for a boy she'd only been with for three weeks.

Beth cared for the men she dated, and there was often a disappointment when the relationship ended. Maybe it was the artist in her. She expected love to feel like more than fondness at the beginning and discontentment at the end. She believed in the rush of emotion talked about in romance novels, of soul mates and happily ever after. She believed in two pieces fitting together, in fate, in there being one person, and in dying from a broken heart.

Maura thought pain and passion were the keys to art. How did one find that? If Beth knew where love hid, she would have sought it out. No one chose to be alone.

So if not love where could she find her passion? In fear? That was much easier to locate. It lived everywhere, and she could seek it out whenever she wanted—dark inlets off the French Quarter, behind construction tarps on the sidewalks, abandoned roads, and haunted farms that were falling in on themselves. There was fear anytime a person had to face mortality. Though, going out and looking for danger in the name of some elusive artistic ideal seemed stupid. Or perhaps Maura was full of nonsense wrapped in an overconfident package, and there was no secret to unlocking Beth's inner elite artist.

Beth drove through town, taking turns through the French Quarter as if on autopilot. She started to go home but then changed her mind. She circled around a block to head back to the shared office space to collect her paintings and hide them, only to change her mind yet again and go back around to go home. She slowed as an SUV pulled out of metered parking. The green light flashed indicating there was still time left on the meter which at three dollars an hour for downtown parking was too good of a deal to pass up. Instead of going home, she took the spot and reached into the back seat for her camera.

If she went home, she would only stress about what Maura said until she drove herself to madness or to tears. Tonight would be a perfect night to get some shots of downtown to sell to the local publications. It would take her mind off the harsh critique.

The crisp air was unusual for this time of year, and she needed a jacket and scarf. The familiar pull of the camera's neck strap was comforting, as she took off the lens cap. Beth checked the meter, seeing she had less than two hours before she had to return to her car. Or she could risk no one noticing the meter ran out before the "free" hours kicked in.

She'd walked these sidewalks several times and had countless pictures of the location. For this reason, she ignored the obvious photos. She did not need more of Bourbon Street's sign, or the many historical balconies and buildings.

She followed the crowd, watching the amorous couples and groups of college students, all pressed together in one big moving mass. She took a few shots, stopping to introduce herself and write down the names of those in the photo. The sound of jazz drifted from various locations, one of the many cultural backdrops she loved about the city.

As she moved through Dutch Alley, she noticed a man sitting alone on a bench by the statue of a Victorian-era woman holding a fruit basket. It wasn't unusual for tourists to take their picture in pretend conversation with the bronze figure, arms draped over her shoulders, hands reaching into her fruit basket as if to steal one. What struck Beth about the man sitting on the bench was that no one was taking his picture, and he seemed to be in a real conversation. He had no earpiece to indicate a phone call.

Beth glanced around and noticed a few of the college kids pointing and laughing. They'd seen the strange interaction, too. She automatically lifted her camera and approached like she'd been taking his photograph all along. The college kids went on their way to look at the artistic wares for sale from the local art Co-Op.

Beth found inspiration in the ruggedly handsome man sitting on the bench next to the statue. Something was mesmerizing about him. She needed to capture that moment, that unguarded expression on his face as he talked to the Victorian woman like she could hear him and give him advice.

Beth turned her full attention to the man's face, focusing on him through the lens. Her finger twitched, but she didn't take the photo as she watched him. What were the odds on the same day she received the advice to seek out her passion that she'd run into the strange tourist again? She studied his face, mentally comparing it to the blurred photo she had from Oxford.

The man had a stoic expression, one that did not give much away. Broad shoulders and thick chest made her think he was used to hard labor. His dark jeans, long t-shirt, and jacket were clean but faded and were nothing like the outfit he'd been wearing in the first photograph. Everything about him signified intensity, from his facial expressions to the way he gestured.

Beth held her breath. It was him. She was sure of it now. She crept closer and kept her camera lifted. This time the photos she took would not be by accident.

6

FAMILIARITY HAD NOT PROVIDED Ivar with much comfort. He had learned the streets of New Orleans as well as the streets of downtown Oxford. Each time he went to Oxford, he walked through the alleyway by the black door. He would touch the wall to feel the texture of the brick against his fingers and then hold his breath in the hope that the portal would appear. It never did.

"I am to drive to Oxford again," Ivar said to the female statue sitting on the bench next to him. The sound of his voice was hoarse because he hadn't spoken for a long time.

It was not lost on him that the only people he felt he could talk to were made of metal. There was this woman, whose name he didn't know. She appeared indifferent to his words. That was all right. The day he thought she actually cared what he said, was the day he'd fall completely into insanity. Then there was good old stationary William Faulkner in Oxford. He always had an ear to listen since that first night Ivar became stranded on Earth.

For the first six weeks, he had practically lived in the alley, huddled in a corner as he waited for rescue. It had not been a pleasant time. At night, he slept in nearby trees, shifted into cat form for comfort. He'd been so hungry and tried to ration the cash-money he carried, but it would not have come close to lasting him for a full year.

It was dumb luck that people had seen him and offered food and new clothes. For some reason, they kept saying he must be from Finland, or thereabouts. He found it better not to answer their questions as they would happily fill in their own gaps. So he came to be Ivar Othevar, from Finland, in need of jobs that paid in cash.

Hard work did not deter him, nor did learning to drive. He didn't have an Earth vehicle license, but Toby Carter, the man who paid him, did not seem to mind that detail. Ivar was happy to have something to fill his hours as he bided his time. And he was very glad to have food and shelter.

"How do you deal with the loneliness? Sitting here day after day," he asked his statue friend.

Ivar wished the statue could answer. Instead, he heard a sea of Earth voices. He was able to pick them apart much better than when he first arrived, noticing the different dialects and languages, but that didn't make them familiar. He missed the cadence of his family's voices, of his native language, and the sounds in the shadowed marshes. He had nightmares that he would never hear them again. The fear that settled inside him the day he became trapped had not left.

He did not give into fear, but it was there, a constant reminder each time he felt his heart beat or his lungs fill with air. Not only did he have to be ready to leave at the right time, someone from the other side had to open the portal to let him in. Someone would. They had to. Surely his people would send that woman he'd pushed through back home. The guilt about that had not left him. He hated that action, but the instinct to protect his home had been deep.

There was no one else to talk to as he searched the streets for dragons. It's not like he could ask if anyone saw a shifter or a gateway to another world. The one time he'd tried delicately to inquire, the man had attempted to punch him before running away in fright. Ivar found most of his conversations usually ended poorly, and it was better to say nothing. Thus, he had his statue friends.

"I might have found a clue to the dragons' whereabouts," he said. "It is rumored that bayou lizard men live in the swamps near here. I might be wasting my efforts, but it is time I expanded my search beyond this city. I have been all over the French Quarter, Treme, really more neighborhoods than I can count. However, I noticed some Draig markings on a brick wall near here that indicates the shadowed marshes. I may not be back to see you for a while."

The statue's expression remained unchanged as if contemplating Ivar's words.

"I know. They are dragons, and they will not be pleased to see a Var prince, but they are from my homeland. They might have access to another portal location." Ivar sighed. "Finn and I knew what would happen at that assembly with the elders. Lord Montague wants the portal destroyed, buried under a mountain so deep no one will ever find it again."

The statue seemed to stare into the distance as if ignoring him. A prickling sensation came over his senses. He narrowed his eyes, concentrating on the intrinsic warning. It had been a long time since he'd felt such apprehension. He wasn't the only shifter on the streets this night. The excitement caused his hands to shake. Was he about to make contact with the dragons? He didn't let on that he felt another shifter approach as he continued talking to the metal woman.

"Yes, that would be bad. I have to believe my parents will not let that happen. I need to go home. I can't stay here. I miss the smells of the shadowed marshes. I have been craving roasted baudron. It is only found in the northern hunting grounds on Draig territory, but my brother and I have gained permission to hunt there many times."

The sensation grew. Shifters were close. He didn't pay attention to his words as he used his sensitive hearing to search through the crowds for his native language.

"But the portal is on Draig territory," Ivar reasoned. "What if the dragon elders use my disappearance as the excuse they need to close off all travel? I know my father. He will not let it stand. It will not look good that Finn came back without me. My parents will start a war to get me back." He took a deep breath, feeling the stress in his stomach that never went away. When he didn't hear anything to prove a shifter was near, he glanced around without trying to be obvious. He felt as if he was being observed. "If the portal is sealed, how will I find a way back home? Alien visitors? They don't come to Earth often, and when they do they stay hidden. First contact hasn't been officially established, and may not be for some time."

A man stumbled by, reeking of liquor and mumbling, "Damn woman broke my heart. If she had married me, I wouldn't be the broken man I am today. It's not my fault. It's not my fault. I should find her and tell her that it's not my fault."

"No offense," Ivar whispered, "but this planet doesn't have much to offer the universe yet. I guess it will be at least another hundred to two-hundred years until aliens make themselves known."

A small clicking noise caught his attention, and he turned to see a woman pointing a camera at him. It hid her face from view. She stood on the other side of the walkway. Dark brown hair with hints of red fell over her shoulders. She wore a white skirt that flared around her legs, leaving the calves bare. A memory tried to surface. She looked familiar.

Was that the presence he'd been feeling? Was this who put his senses on alert? She did capture his notice.

Her blue shirt hugged her figure, revealing each

feminine curve. Tension rolled over him when she didn't turn away. His eyes narrowed as he focused on her, trying to figure out what she was doing to him.

It was the woman in white. The one from the first day he arrived. He'd found her again. But why now? And why did she bring with her a feeling of warning?

No, there were others here too. Shifters. Why did they come now? On the night he found her again.

Ivar had looked for her after that first evening, each time he was downtown in Oxford to check the portals. He'd never thought to look for her in New Orleans.

Like last time, seeing her made the beast want to come out and play. Her finger twitched, and the click happened again. It was as if she purposefully made every primal instinct he had surge forth.

She lowered the camera from her face and slowly stepped back. Her eyes met and held his.

"It is her," Ivar whispered to the statue. "The one I told you about. The one the gods sent to show me what I could not have."

He was too afraid to move scared she'd vanish. But there was another fear, the creeping one in the back of his mind, the knowledge that he was not the only shifter roaming the streets. Movement caught his attention, followed by the flash of glowing eyes.

Dragon.

No, not just a single dragon. There were two of them, possibly more. He saw them glaring at him from within the nearby shadows. There was nothing friendly about their expressions. He wasn't surprised. He hadn't expected them to give him a warm welcome. They had to suspect he wanted them to go home. Still, he was a prince, and they should not have been threatening him. Ivar wanted to do this peacefully.

Ivar stood, a growl stuck in his throat. His body threatened with a shift. The woman's eyes widened, and she stumbled. She must have seen the dragons, too.

She took off running as if chased by rabid yorkins, or in this case angry dragons. Ivar jumped to his feet and glanced around, trying to see who threatened her. The dragons had disappeared into the shadows. Were they chasing her? Not seeing an attacker, Ivar ran after the woman, intent on protecting her.

7

BETH RUSHED through the crowd only stopping when she was through Dutch Alley. Part of her expected there to be panic in the streets. How could no one have seen what she had? A demon loose in New Orleans? Or a vampire? What else would have eyes with a supernatural glow?

Well, actually, the people of New Orleans would probably welcome a vampire.

Beth stopped running and pressed close to a building. She searched the crowd, not seeing anyone coming for her. Rumors flooded the city of para-normal and supernatural creatures, but she'd always taken that as local lore to sell ghost tour tickets to the tourists. Never in a million years would she have guessed it was real.

And she'd captured proof.

Beth lifted her camera to study the viewing screen on the back. She enlarged the last photo of the man as much as she could. It was hard to tell on the smaller screen, but she would have sworn his eyes glowed. Not the captured reflection of streetlights like in the first photograph from Oxford could have been, but a genuinely bioluminescent glow from within. A strange shadow marred the sides of his eyes. The orange color contrast made little sense, but the camera screen only let her zoom in so much.

Had she really captured a vampire?

It was night, and he was mesmerizingly handsome. Broad shoulders and thick muscles molded beneath tight flesh. He wore snug denim jeans and a dark jacket. She felt a sexual ping in her stomach when she looked at him. Wait, vampires didn't have a reflection, right? So could they have their pictures taken? Or was that just Hollywood nonsense?

A memory nagged at the back of her mind. What had those kids said the night she took the first photo? Cat-man? It had been a passing amusement at the time, but maybe there was something to that conversation. Was the orange distortion really fur? She could have sworn one of the college boys said tiger. Had the photo from Mississippi somehow not been the perfect combination of special effect lighting and movement and instead was a supernatural cat-man? That wasn't any more believable than a vampire.

Beth turned the dial on the camera, flipping through the digital files. She stared at the first photo of the man as he talked to the statue. With each new photo, she watched as he turned toward her. His smile dropped, and his expression intensified as he peered into the camera.

Beth stared at the evidence. Her hands shook as she moved to the next photo. Eyes began to glow, and his face changed. He'd stood, the movement of his body sure and fluid as he'd tried to come after her.

What should she do? Should she tell someone? Who would believe her? Did she even believe herself? If she showed anyone the photo, they would assume it was a fake. That is what she would have thought if someone said they had evidence of a supernatural creature.

She hadn't planned her escape very well. To reach her car, she needed to cross Dutch Alley and go in the other direction. That meant chancing another encounter. He'd looked at her with those penetrating eyes. Surely he knew she'd seen his transformation.

She debated on how to proceed. If she took the

side streets, there might not be many people, but then she'd be a woman walking alone in the dark with a supernatural being on the loose. Her parking meter ran out in a half hour, but paying for parking wasn't required after 7pm. Maybe she could duck into a bar and hide until the last call.

What if there were more of them? How many supernatural creatures could be running wild in the French Quarter? Beth looked around, fighting the urge to run. Her thoughts were a scattered mess. No one had the mystique of Mr. Glowing Green Eyes, but that didn't mean there weren't more of them out there. Her heart beat harder than it should have.

"Oh, dammit, this is stupid," she whispered before holding on to her camera and sprinting down the sidewalk. Beth didn't care how crazy she looked, running with no one chasing her. She couldn't force herself to look around as she made a beeline straight to her car. Home would be safer than out in the open.

She pulled her keys from where they hung attached to her camera strap and tapped the button to unlock the door. As she slid into the driver's seat, she took several deep breaths. The sound was audible as she turned on the ignition.

The headlights exposed a dark corner. She gasped, seeing an orange tiger sitting in the dark, staring at her. Cat-man was real. The beast didn't move. The idea that she'd ran past it caused her breathing to speed up. She shook as she put the car into gear. The motor must have made a sound because the cat took off between two buildings.

Beth slowly drove past the opening, trying to see the cat. Instead, she saw the silhouette of a large man. He stood as if staring at her from within the shadows. It looked as if he held a pair of jeans in his hand. Was he naked in that alley?

"Cat-man," she whispered, terrified that she might be hallucinating. Nothing made sense. She wanted desperately to go home to find a reasonable explanation, and at the same time, she knew there wasn't one.

Whoever he was, he silently summoned her closer. She had the urge to get out of the car and run to him. It took everything in her to step on the gas and speed away.

8

BETH COULDN'T STOP her hands from shaking as she tried forcing the key into the lock of her apartment door. It took longer than it should have and in the end the door opened without her key. She stood in the doorway, her breath held and eyes wide as she looked inside at a lamp she had not left on. She started to leave.

"Beth, is that you?"

Beth squeaked in fright at the sound but then she realized it was her neighbor, Yvonne Davies.

"I tried calling you earlier. I hope you don't mind that I let myself in. I found my mail in the basket." Yvonne had been raised in the South, but extensive traveling when she was younger had neutralized her

Southern accent to what Beth thought of as Southern-light.

Beth glanced at the wicker basket, seeing it was still filled with the woman's catalogs and envelopes. She slid her photography portfolio on the small table close to the door and set her camera bag on the floor. In her panic to get inside, she barely remembered grabbing them. It must have been an automatic response.

"Why didn't you tell me you found that delectable man from your photo?" Yvonne insisted.

He was there?

"Yvonne," Beth whispered, inching from the front door toward her living room. Fear choked her, and she could barely get the words out. "I need you to run. It's not safe."

"It is very high fantasy compared to what you normally do," Yvonne continued, clearly not hearing the warning.

Beth peeked around the corner. Yvonne moved across the small apartment, looking from painting to painting, studying them as if they were hanging in a gallery when in fact they were propped up against a wall on Beth's floor.

Beth sighed in relief. Yvonne was only looking at her paintings.

"Please tell me you're at least dating this man," Yvonne said, indicating the fact each painting had versions of the same subject. She wondered what Maura would have said about this peculiar hodge-podge of artistic styles.

When Beth obsessively painted the handsome face she hadn't known he was a cat-man. She also didn't expect anyone else would see the collection.

"When can I meet him?" Yvonne asked.

"He's just..." What could she say? "I don't know who he is. I made him up."

If not for the pictures she'd seen on her camera, she would have thought the cat-man was a hallucination. The first image had mesmerized her, but these paintings were nothing she thought of showing other people. She looked at it as more of a way to practice her techniques.

"Seriously, why haven't I seen these before?" Yvonne used the tip of her finger to pull back a canvas to see what was behind it.

Had Beth known her neighbor was coming home a day early, she would have hidden them in her room. "When the muse hits, it must be obeyed."

Yvonne pulled out a close up of the man's face. "This one. This is my favorite. The lighting in his eyes is very unusual."

The color hues were unnatural for human skin tones. But, then, she'd painted his flesh with orange, white, and black while giving his skin a smooth texture. At the time, she'd mimicked the strange colors that appeared on the original photo. Only now did she realize it was a blending of man and tiger, no fur, no fangs, but the intensity she'd seen in his gaze. The painting had haunted her dreams, and so she'd hidden it, that way the man could not stare at her when she walked around her apartment. Now, knowing about the cat-man, the image somehow seemed dead on perfect.

"How was Japan?" Beth asked, not wanting to be alone. She went to the window and peeked outside at the street below. Someone walked past but didn't seem threatening. She watched as he made his way down the sidewalk.

"We went to a bar where we were served drinks by two adorable macaque monkeys. They took our orders and delivered them," Yvonne said. "Which reminds me, I brought you something. It's by the door."

Beth found the yellow gift bag and reached inside. A red silk robe with delicately embroidered cherry blossoms slid against her hands as she lifted it. "Thank you, it's beautiful."

"How did your meeting go at the gallery?" Yvonne asked. "When was that happening again?"

"Today. Maura Masters said I had potential, but that the collection wasn't edgy enough for her."

"You evidently didn't show this one to her?" Yvonne lifted the portrait of the cat-man and held it before Beth. "Take this down to Ron's studio and catch her before she leaves town."

"I don't know." Beth again crossed to the window and searched the street below. "I'm not sure I'm going to show it. As you said, it's very science fiction and—"

"Don't be silly," Yvonne scolded. "They're all good, but this one is transcendent."

"Yeah, maybe," she answered, distracted.

"Are you waiting on a date?" Yvonne sounded excited. She hurried to the window to look out. "Who is he?"

"No one," Beth dismissed. "I thought I saw a stray cat outside and was watching for it."

"I'm a dog person myself," Yvonne said, as she went to gather her mail from the basket. "But I think you taking in a pet is a great idea. You shouldn't be alone in here by yourself painting all the time."

"You make it sound like I'm some kind of crazy recluse who never leaves the house," Beth chuckled.

"More old maid than a recluse," Yvonne teased. "You can't date a paintbrush."

"But it can still break your heart," Beth answered, looking at the cat-man's face on canvas. "I'm not looking for a boyfriend. I need to focus on my career first. I can't have any distractions right now."

"So you've said," Yvonne mumbled with a disbelieving smirk.

Yvonne said something more before leaving, but Beth wasn't sure if she actually answered the woman or said goodbye. To know that her vision had come to life was surreal. It was the perfect convergence of an accidental photo, the playful conversation of college kids, and the unlikely odds of seeing the same man in two different cities.

A knock sounded on the door, and Beth moved to answer it. "Yvonne? Did you forget something—?" Her words ended with a sharp gasp.

Cat-man stood staring at her. His chest heaved as if he'd run up the stairs to her second story apartment. How did he find her? And why? She stumbled away from the door.

"You are safe." The words were gruff, and the tone of his voice made her feel anything but.

She reached around, blindly feeling for a weapon. She couldn't look away. Though all the pertinent areas were covered, he was bare-chested and held his shirt in his hand. Her fingers met something, and she grabbed it, holding it up in warning.

"I surveyed the alleyway. You were not followed. You are safe," he said.

He didn't come inside, and she slowly lowered her hand. It was only then she realized she had been about to defend herself with a wicker basket. She dropped it, and he surged forward with lightning fast reflexes. Beth inhaled sharply and stumbled away from him, lifting her arms in defense. Instead of harming her, he caught the basket before it hit the floor and held it out for her to take.

Trembling, she took the basket from him and set it beside her feet on the floor. His earnest eyes watched her expectantly, and he didn't move. The cat-man stayed kneeling on the floor. Nothing about his demeanor was threatening unless she counted the fact that he was more magnetically gorgeous than any man had a right to be. Knowing the power he had, the ability to become a tiger, a tiger that she had seen staring at her in the alleyway, should have made her scream and run. Instead, she stood, breathing hard, unable to look away.

"Who...?" she finally managed.

"Who?" He repeated, slowly pushing to his feet.

She really wished he had stayed down. When he stood, it became apparent just how tall and broad he was. "I do not know who was after you, but I assume you saw the dragons? I don't think they followed you. Are they after you? Do you know something about where they are hiding?"

"Uh...?" She wasn't sure what to say to his rush of questions. "Dragons? Is that a gang?"

"They are a group, yes. But do not worry. You are safe. I checked the alleyway. A man was sleeping. I gave him money for food and asked him to please leave the area for his own safety, but he appeared harmless."

"Who are you?" she asked, not taking her eyes off him.

"Forgive me. I am Pr..." He hesitated and looked down at the floor. "I am called Ivar Othevar. And you?"

"Beth—Bethany Watson. Call me Beth. What are you?" Her throat was so tight. She could barely breathe, but at least the words were coming faster now.

"Beth. I am a..." Again he hesitated, glancing up at her before looking back down. "I am a driver of trucks. I take a route between Oxford and New Orleans."

"You're a cat." Beth lifted her hand toward the paintings but still didn't take her eyes from him. "I saw you in the alley when I got into my car. That was you, right? You're the cat-man."

He moved to look where she gestured. Seeing the paintings, he stared at them. She studied his bare back for movement. The solid lines of muscles along his spine flexed. She didn't know why she wasn't scared, but she suddenly felt safe.

"You did this?" he asked, not looking away. "Have you been following me? Is that why you are in this city, too?"

"I live here. I took a picture of you while visiting Oxford last year. It was an accident. I didn't even know I had taken it until after I came home and was going through my files. I hope you don't mind. I took some artistic liberties. There was something sad and determined in your expression." Beth had stared at that photo for hours, trying to interpret the emotions. Never had she imagined she would be staring at him, standing shirtless no less, in her living room.

He didn't move.

"And then tonight..." She finally looked away long enough to grab her camera bag from beside the door. When she turned back, she almost ran into his chest. She hadn't even heard him move.

Agile like a cat, she thought with a tiny shiver.

"I saw..." She wasn't sure how to say it. "I saw a tiger and then you in the alley. You can change, can't you? Shift your shape from one form to another?"

He looked as if he might deny it but then nodded once.

"How can...? I mean, how do you...?" Beth wanted to touch him, to see if this was a hallucination. If someone said they saw men who shifted into cats, she'd have been one of the first to get them professional psychiatric help. "I'm sorry, I have always believed in the possibility of there being more out there, like ghosts being transferred energy at the time of death or psychic abilities developing in people who use a higher percentage of their brain, but I'm finding it very hard to believe in shape-shifting."

Without warning, Ivar's body started to change. Fur sprouted along his features, running from his face down his chest. Claws extended from his fingertips and his eyes began to glow. For several deep breaths, he stood as a man-cat before the transformation continued. His body trembled violently as he bent over. She watched his form contract, pressing into the shape of a large tiger as if his cells somehow shrunk to fit the new frame. The jeans slid from his feline hips. He stepped toward her, head lowered. She lifted her hand to gesture at him to stop, and he placed his head against her palm. The softness of his fur took her by surprise, not that fur was soft, but that it was real. She touched him longer than she should have, hesitantly petting him as if he were a domesticated animal.

Fur grew, changing into longer hair. She felt the shift beneath her hand as the locks tangled around her fingers. He looked up at her, cat eyes turning more human, paws growing into hands. The fur receded as if it had never been. The man knelt before her.

Naked.

He knelt before her naked.

Beth realized her hand was still in his hair and she jerked back. Her skin tingled as if he'd done something magical to her. The lamplight cast over him, giving an appealing view of his flesh. The soft yellow tint of the bulb fused against his skin like sculpted granite, carved by the hand of a Renaissance master. She averted her eyes. "You should put your clothes on."

She heard the sound of his movement and hoped —*didn't hope?*—he complied.

When the sounds behind her stopped, she

waited a few more seconds before peeking over her shoulder. He stood, completely dressed. He'd even put on his shirt.

"Do you find it easier to believe now that you have seen?" he asked.

"Does it hurt?" Beth wasn't sure why she asked that out of all the questions she could have come up with. She imagined what it might feel like to have her body crushed and molded into a new shape.

"No." He shook his head. "It does not cause me pain."

"Are there more cat-people?" Beth's mind raced. She wasn't sure why this man was standing in her apartment like her artistic muse come to life. Maybe she was crazy? She heard stories of mental patients living in their own world but actually were in a hospital somewhere. That explanation sounded more plausible than a shifter in her living room.

"Yes." He nodded once.

"There are cat-shifters in New Orleans?" How did no one know about this?

"I do not think so. I have looked, but I have not found cat-shifters here."

"Is it rude of me to ask these questions?" Beth wanted to touch him again, so she pulled her hands together and held them in front of her stomach. "I didn't mean to make it sound like I thought you were some kind of sideshow curiosity. It's just... *Wow*, you know."

"You should ask questions if you have them." His eyes strayed to the picture she'd painted of him.

"Do you have questions for me?" Beth couldn't imagine what he'd have to ask her, but it seemed polite to at least offer.

"May I see this photo you said you took of me in Oxford?"

"Of course." Beth crossed to her portfolio and laid it on her small dining table. She flipped through the pages before finding what she was looking for. She gestured down at it. "Here."

Ivar stepped closer to her, and she felt the heat radiating off his body. She smelled the subtle scent he wore, soap and something else she couldn't define. This couldn't be a delusion. It felt too real. But if it was a delusion, did that mean she could lift her hand and touch his hair again? If this weren't real, then it wouldn't matter, would it?

"I remember this night," he said after a long moment. "It was the night I arrived. I saw you across the street with what I thought was a magical device."

"Magical device?"

"Camera." He gave a small laugh. "I have learned much since then."

"You saw me take your picture? I didn't see you."

"A man bumped into you. He had funny white facial hair." Ivar gestured to his face to indicate a long mustache. "I have not seen the style since."

"I vaguely remember that happening. It was an extraordinary night. College kids were talking about a cat-man. Some guy was walking around asking people to marry him." Beth looked at the photo as if it could unlock the past.

"You saw Finn?" This news seemed to excite him.

"Yes." She slowly nodded. "I think he said that was his name. Do you know him?"

Ivar's eyes flashed with green briefly before disappearing beneath his closed lids. He nodded once.

"In that picture, what were you running from?" She inched closer to him. The floorboards creaked, and his eyes opened. The glow was gone.

"I wasn't running from anything."

"What were you chasing?" Beth studied his expression, staring as he looked at his photo. In some ways, she'd lived with his face for months, and that made him feel like a friend, but she had to remind herself that he was a stranger who had come to her home less than an hour ago.

"You. I was trying to get to you."

The answer was honest, simple, and she didn't know what to do with it. It thrilled and frightened her at the same time. She found herself leaning closer. "Because of a magic camera?"

He shook his head. "Because I was lost, and when I saw you I didn't feel as lost."

Beth's breath caught as he turned to face her. He stood close. There was something almost lover-like in the way he regarded her. She'd be a fool not to admit the chemistry she felt, a magnetic pull to be near him. But physical attraction aside, she wasn't in the market for a boyfriend. She had a plan. A good plan that involved establishing herself as an artist. "Where do you think the other cat-shifters are if they are not here?"

"I know they are on Qurilixen. I have been searching for the Draig in this city, but I have been unable to locate them until tonight."

"Draig?"

"Dragon-shifters," he explained.

"Dragon-*shifters*?" Is that what he'd meant when he said the dragons had been following her? This night kept getting stranger with each passing moment. Cats were one thing. She had seen a tiger before. But for some reason, the idea of mythological dragons was a little harder to believe.

"Yes." He nodded. "Dragon-shifters come from the same place as my people."

She felt he was telling the truth but didn't know exactly what to do with the information. She also wasn't sure which questions to ask next. "I don't understand why you are telling me all of this. Why are shifters interested in me? I'm just... *me*."

"I'm telling you because you asked." His eyes dipped to her mouth as if he wanted to kiss her. For an insane moment, she thought about letting him.

"You were lost in Oxford when I happened to be visiting there. And now you are in New Orleans looking for dragons." Beth shook her head and backed away. What was she doing? This whole evening was insanity. She had the urge to lock herself in her bathroom and hide in the bathtub where no one would think to look for her until morning. "Is this some kind of joke? I mean that's a lot of coincidences. I don't know who would want to prank me like this, but..."

Ivar stepped back as if she had somehow insulted him with her observation. "I don't question what the gods have planned. I did that once, and it did not end well for me. They sent me to you, and I will not fail to understand what I must do." He went to the window and looked out. "Something is not right. What do the dragons want from you? They did not appear until I saw you."

"What do you mean the dragons want me? Why would anyone want me? I'm just an artist. My last art critique was earlier today, and it was brutal if I'm honest about it, so it's possible I'm not even a note-worthy artist."

At that, he frowned. "Then you must stop talking to people who do not understand art." He gestured at the painting of his face. "You captured something I have not wanted to face within myself."

There was a conviction in his voice, and he complimented her more with that one declaration than she'd received in a lifetime. "Why are the dragons after me? What do they want?"

"You tell me. You ran from them." He again looked out the window.

"No. I ran from you. I saw your eyes change when you were on the bench next to the Victorian lady statue, and I panicked." She went to see what he looked at. "Are there dragons outside right now?"

"You can't sense them?" He frowned before answering his own question. "Of course you can't.

You're an Earth human. If you know nothing about this, they must be here for me. This is more than I wanted to say to you tonight, but I found the dragon-shifters. Or, more to the point, I think they found me. There is a chance they will not be happy with my presence. They defected from Qurilixen, and they know I'll want to take them back to our home planet with me. They might not be willing to return."

"Planet?" As in alien cat-shifter capturing dragon-shifters visiting Earth? Every time she began to feel as if she might be sane, he'd say something else that made her believe otherwise. "What exactly did you mean when you stated that you arrived the night I took that picture?"

"That was the night Finn and I came through the portal to visit Earth." He said the words, yet he managed to keep a straight face.

"*Sooo*," she drew out her words as if to prompt the punch line that hadn't been forthcoming. "Is this, um, your first time, ah, visiting us?"

"No. We have come before through the portals. Until recently, though, they were sealed, and travel was forbidden. Our ancestors used them to escape from Earth long ago, and now we use them to come here and look for brides."

"Oh, yeah?" Even to her own ears, her voice sounded abnormally high in her disbelief.

"Yes." He nodded, not seeming to notice the fact she was inching further and further away from him. He smiled. "It is nice to be able to talk about this to a living person. Portal travel is a very political matter on my planet."

"Of course. I think it would be." Her eyes were wide as she nodded. *I'm not crazy. I'm not crazy. This guy is crazy. I may be crazy.*

"The shifter elders remember what it was like when your people tried to hunt us to extinction."

"We did that?" She slowly sat down on a small bar stool, letting the crazy just play itself out. This was almost too much.

"Yes. There are a few elders left who used to live on Earth who have told us the stories. Religious zealots spread fear about anything that was supernatural. They called us evil. Cats and dragons made an alliance. We left together through the portal and buried the opening inside a mountain so humans could not follow us. The intent was never to return."

"But you did return." Each time he paused, she felt compelled to speak. Beth told herself to be quiet, to not encourage him.

"It would seem the gods had other plans for us,

and we were obligated to come back. Shifter females stopped being born, and without humans, there is no source of compatible mates for my people—at least not in the numbers we need for long-term survival."

"So you're here to..." She didn't bother to finish the sentence. Her eyes strayed to a bottle of vodka on her kitchen counter. She rarely drank, but she contemplated reaching for the liquor now.

"Finn and I came to find brides to stop the elders from sealing off the portal at the next royal assembly. They were to take a vote, but the outcome was inevitable. So, we took action to keep the portals open until we could find another way to supply brides to shifter men."

"And why would your coming here keep them open?"

"If the elders saw us happily married, then they would be forced to change their minds." He sighed heavily. He again checked the window. "Finn and I are princes. If they didn't leave them open, the single men still looking for mates would force their hand. To close the portals only after the princes found wives would send a bad message to the people."

Cat-shifters. Dragon-shifters. Aliens. Portals. Princes. Insanity.

"Come. We should leave this place." He moved

as if he expected her to follow him out the apartment door.

Beth stood from the stool.

"Um..." She followed him, but instead of going into the hall after him, she shut the door and locked the deadbolt. "No."

9

IVAR TENSED as the door swung shut and then slammed behind him. The click of the lock seemed to drive home the fact that Beth hadn't followed him, instead she was still inside and he, outside.

He reached for the doorknob, testing it. It was locked. "Beth?"

She didn't answer.

"Beth, are you safe?"

Ivar pressed his ear to the door and focused his hearing. He heard the sound of footsteps and the clinking of ice in a glass. Liquid poured. He didn't understand.

It was fairly obvious that the gods wanted him to be with this woman. He'd seen her the first night he was trapped, felt compelled to go to her before she disappeared. His intentions to claim any woman were not the most honorable in hindsight. Apparently, the gods had wanted him to wait for the right one. But tonight, when he saw her again, he knew. She was meant to be with him. He had to protect her. He had to keep her safe.

Mated shifter men all explained love the same way. One look, one moment, and a man knew whom he was meant to spend eternity with. He felt it that first night. He felt it now. It was as much a part of him as shifting and breathing. It was fate. And Ivar's fate was named Beth.

So why in all the blasted forests was she not following him to safety?

The gods were not going to make this easy on him.

Ivar pressed his ear closer to the door. Nothing. He looked to the floor seeing two shadows the size of feet. He leaned and looked inside the peephole. Beth gasped on the other side, and the shadows disappeared as she moved away.

"Beth?" Ivar knocked on the door. "Do you need time to prepare for the journey?"

She was beautiful, so much more than he'd remembered. When he'd knelt before her, gazing up in the soft light after she'd stroked his head, it had taken everything in him to resist wrapping her in his arms to kiss her. The animal inside of him wanted to play. The man inside him had to put a tight leash on the big cat. Ripping off his mate's clothing wasn't exactly honorable, at least not during their first conversation.

Well, unless she wanted him to.

Ivar's grin only lasted a few seconds. His senses tingled. He'd momentarily forgotten the dragons on the street below. He looked down the dimly lit hallway. The building was old and had a faint musky smell. It was not the place he wanted his princess to live. Beth deserved palaces and exquisite gowns. He wanted to give them to her.

"I told you." The Draig voice was unmistakable as was his use of the Qurilixian language.

"Yes, but is it *him*?" another voice answered. "Where is his guard?"

Ivar moved toward the sound. Sternly, he ordered, "Make yourselves known."

Seconds later, a door cracked open, and a woman glanced into the hall. Seeing Ivar, she slammed it shut.

"I told you they would hunt us down, Galen," the first voice stated. "It is just as we were warned. They won't let us find happiness. They want us at their mercy."

"Galen of the Draig?" Ivar stated more than asked. "I know your name. You were among some of the first to sneak through the portal. You and your brother, Seanan. Is that who is with you?"

The dragons didn't answer.

"I know who you are," Ivar said. "Why did you leave? By all accounts, you were a loyal and trusted member of the Draig guard."

"It's Galen Flaherty now. My brother did not sneak through. He was the first to go through and was stranded. I came to find him when the royals failed to do so."

"And is that your brother with you?" Ivar asked.

"Sean is not here," Galen said. "Leave him alone. He's happy where he is, and I'll never tell you where to find him."

"Who is with you?" Ivar narrowed his eyes.

There was a pause, before someone answered, "You may call me Jerry."

"Are you Draig?" Ivar frowned. Jerry of the Draig didn't sound like a name he'd ever heard of.

"We make our own lives here," Jerry answered. "I am Cajun now."

"Cajun?" Ivar tried to place where he might have heard that word before.

"Ursa performed the ceremony to welcome us," Jerry said. "We are Cajun now, not Draig."

Ivar had no idea what they were talking about. Had time on Earth driven them mad? Ivar could understand if it had.

"We make our own tribe," Galen said, "and no longer live under the rule of Draig."

"Do you know who I am?" Ivar continued down the hall, following the sound of the voices.

"You're one of the cat-shifter princes. I saw you visit with your family when I worked at the palace." Galen stepped out of the shadows. "But this is not your dominion, and we are not your royal subjects even if it was. What are you doing on Earth?"

Ivar heard movement behind him and didn't answer. He willed whoever it was to go back into their apartment.

"We don't recognize your authority," Jerry stepped from the shadows. Whereas Galen appeared almost puzzled, Jerry was aggressive. "You should not have come to the city of plague."

"What is the city of plague?" Ivar dared a step closer. He wanted to lead them away from Beth's door.

"You have seen the streets out there, have you not?" Jerry motioned around as if to encompass the city. "Surely you have witnessed the trials the humans face here. They are most horrible."

"Ursa said they are not plagued," Galen corrected. "They are lost."

"Call it what you will," Jerry said, "but I have seen them dancing in the streets, screaming and running, laughing as they watch their friends spill their insides onto the sidewalks."

"Where are your guards?" Galen demanded, turning the conversation back to Ivar. He lifted his hand as if to calm his friend. "We know they would not send you alone."

"You're right. They would not." Ivar wasn't about to tell them his situation, not with this rude welcome he was receiving.

"Where are they hiding? We've been following you for months." Jerry took a hostile step forward.

"I've been searching for you." There was no point in lying. If they had indeed been following him, they knew he was alone. He did not live like a prince on Earth. And he could use their help to get home. They knew where the New Orleans portal was and when it might open—that is if the Draig guards didn't block travel that night.

Galen held Jerry back. "Has something happened on Qurilixen, prince? Is that why you are here?"

"Your leaving has caused significant controversy," Ivar said. "The elders have been threatening to close the portals permanently. We are trying to stop them. You must return with me and tell the others they are not to come here without guidance. They must see that you are alive and that you chose to come home over staying here. Travel must be regulated so that others do not end up in cities of plague."

"It is as we feared," Jerry stated. "He's here to force us to go back."

Ivar heard movement behind him and turned to the side to see both directions down the hall. Dragons appeared from behind a corner, filling the space to block off his escape. He growled in warning. Jerry and Galen charged forward. Ivar put up his fists, not expecting the attack. The narrow passage did not offer a way to escape. He spun, automatically making contact with Jerry's jaw. Fur sprouted over his arms, and the shift gave strength to the blow. Jerry flew backward only to right his footing and come back for him.

"Ivar!" Beth opened her door, waving at him to enter.

Ivar pushed one dragon and punched another. They did not go down easily as they struck him in the shoulder and back. Beth screamed in fright. Ivar dove inside her apartment, not so much as to escape but to protect her. He tried to slam the door, but the dragons managed to push their way in.

"This way," Beth yelled.

The panic in her voice caused the beast inside him to fight harder. He felt his claws meet flesh. A dragon cried out. Furniture crashed. Glass broke. One of Beth's paintings of him flew past. It struck one of the dragons on the head.

"Come on," she ordered.

He followed her into a bathroom where she shoved the door closed behind her and pushed the lock.

"Go to the window, there's a ladder." Beth gestured toward the wall behind the claw foot bathtub. She didn't wait for him to go first as she climbed inside and pulled the latch to force open the window. The dragons pounded at the door, causing the wooden frame to groan, as the door seemed to warp with each strike.

Beth braced her foot on the edge of the bathtub and tried to put herself through the window feet first. Ivar braced her waist to help her. She found footing on the other side and motioned that he should follow.

"Come on," she shouted.

It was a tighter fit for him, but he went through head first, using the tub for leverage. He watched her climb down the side of the building to a platform. When she hit the grated walkway and darted to the next level of steps to reach the alley below, he grabbed a ladder rung and held tight. His heart hammered violently, partially from the chase but mostly for fear that something could happen to her. Jumping, he flipped out of the window, swung around, and then released his hands so that he landed at the bottom of the ladder. The sound of breaking wood exploded above them. The dragons were in the bathroom.

"Hurry," she cried, scurrying down a small, rusty stairwell. "My car is this way."

Beth turned back to look at him. Her worried eyes met his for the shortest of moments before her entire body jerked and she began to shake. A strange crackling noise burst over the alley for a few seconds.

Tension left Beth's body, and she collapsed. He darted to catch her, but she never made it to the ground. Hands came from behind to hold her up. Beth moaned.

"Keep her quiet," a man ordered. "We'll take her with us and sort this out later."

Ivar growled. He surged forward to rescue his mate. Two sharp bites hit his back. He tried to go forward, but electrical current flowed through him. Two more bites hit him on the side. He stumbled and collapsed forward onto his hands and knees. Beth moaned lightly.

"He's a strong bastard. Inject him and get him into the truck," the same voice ordered. "We can't do this here."

Ivar growled, fighting through the strange, helpless sensation. A different kind of sharp jab hit his neck. He swiped to stop it but missed. His vision blurred. He tried to block his fall, but the pavement was coming too fast for his face, and his hands were useless.

10

BETH FELT her body being bounced around. The hum of an engine and tires against a dirt road were unmistakable. Her hazed mind made it hard to focus on what was happening. Lights streaked in a blur, but she couldn't tell where they came from. Her hand brushed up against warmth, and it took all her energy to turn her head from one side to the other.

Ivar lay next to her. They were in the back of some vehicle, bouncing on thin blankets like luggage. She moaned softly when she tried to say his name. It was the only sound she could manage. His eyes were closed, but she felt the soft exhale of his breath to her cheek. Very little about this situation made sense, but looking at him made her feel safe. Her hand bumped against his. She was unable to hold him, but the contact was enough for now.

She tried to keep her eyes open, but her vision would not stay focused. Her lids drooped. Maybe she could just rest for a second.

BETH FOCUSED on the wall as she tried to reason where she was. Her muscles were sore as if she'd run a marathon, and her mind was in a drugged haze as if she'd been injected with a tranquilizer. In fact, she was pretty sure that's exactly what had happened. Well, not the marathon part, but definitely drugged.

Framed photographs hung on the wall, showcasing images of a swamp. Spanish moss covered the trees. Alligators peeked out from the murky water. The last picture looked like what could only be a backwater Santa Claus posing on an airboat midjolly laugh. Planked walls appeared to be the inside of a log cabin.

Beth sat on a bed with a blue blanket. A silver dragon was embroidered on the center of it. Beth instantly stood.

"Dragon?" she whispered, grasping memories as

they tried to flood in. "Dragon-shifters are coming. We have to run."

Beth stumbled through the door. She had to do something. She needed to find someone.

"Ivar." Her voice croaked. The cabin only had a few pieces of furniture. It looked more like a hideout than someone's actual home. She listened, hearing only the hum of an old refrigerator.

Nothing about this felt right. She vaguely recalled being in a vehicle, seeing the dim lights streaking over Ivar's still face. The reality of her situation began pressing in on her. She was attacked in her apartment. Men came. She jumped out of the window. No. *They* jumped out of the bathroom window. The men had been after Ivar, and she had been trying to help him.

Beth looked at her shaking hand. An angry red wound throbbed on her palm. She'd cut it on the way down the ladder outside her window.

The dragons had found them in the alley. The last thing she remembered was staring at Ivar's half-shifted face as electricity coursed through her body. The stun gun shouldn't have knocked her out, as that was just some kind of myth from Hollywood movies, but something happened, and her world had gone dark. She felt her head, not feeling a bump that would have knocked her unconscious. Maybe that's when they used the drugs?

"What did I tell you?" a woman yelled in anger. It came from outside. Beth gasped, covering her mouth to try to hide the panting sound of fear. She held very still as a strange murmuring answered the woman. When no one else came into the cabin, she inched toward the front door.

"What? I can't hear you? What are our rules?" the woman demanded.

Beth pressed close to the front door of the cabin. She leaned to look out a small window to take a peek outside. She moved slowly, worried about what she might find. Trees formed a fence on the left edge of a large yard that ran down to the water. In the far right-hand corner, an airboat was moored to a rickety dock with a fishing platform on the end. Where in the world was she?

"Women get to make their own choices," a drone of male voices said, sounding very much like scolded children.

"And...?" the woman insisted.

Beth inched over a little more, finding a woman on the lawn in front of a dozen men. She stood with her feet wide apart as if she were the leader of the group. The men kept their heads bowed before her, glancing up a few times as if worried about becoming the focus of her rage.

Beth recognized a few of the men. These were the dragon men who attacked them. Her mind continued to clear by small degrees but with clarity, came fear. She'd been kidnapped and taken to the swamps by dragon-shifters. What did they want with her? Where was Ivar? How could she escape?

The woman speaking looked about Beth's age and appeared human enough, but what woman bossed around an army of dragon men in the middle of swamp country?

There was a long silence before one of the scolded dragons hesitantly offered, "Wear clothes outside except when Ursa is performing the Cajun ceremony, or we are swimming in the swamp?"

Beth pulled back so they wouldn't see her through the window. They weren't guarding her. Maybe they hadn't expected her to wake up yet. This might be her only chance at escape.

"Don't shift in public?" another man sounded as if he merely guessed at his answer.

"Don't tell people we're from another planet." The new voice had more confidence than the first two.

"This is the South. We are Cajun."

The responses came faster, almost overlapping each other.

"Poisonous snakes aren't good gifts when courting a female."

"Alligators are not shifters."

"Don't eat the wrapper."

"Don't start a conversation with, I would like you to have my twenty sons."

"We don't need to fear the zealots anymore."

"No, we *should* fear the zealots," someone corrected. "They want to kill us."

"No one should say the words dragon and seed together in a sentence, even if we want to fill a woman with our dragon seed. You don't like it, Lori."

"People aren't trying to kill us when they point their fingers."

"Bar fights are bad and—"

"Yes," the woman broke through the barrage of male voices. "All that is true. But we also don't kidnap potential brides."

"But, Lori, she saw—" one man tried to defend.

"No," Lori stated firmly.

"But, she—" he tried again.

"Just no," Lori said, louder.

Beth slowly backed away from the strange turn of the lecture. Grumbles started which sounded like they might be apologies. Maybe the drugs hadn't worn off, and she was hearing things? This hardly seemed like a fierce band of kidnappers.

She moved through the cabin toward the sound of the refrigerator. Her throat was parched, but she didn't stop to drink. A narrow door in the back might be her only chance. She tested the handle, finding it unlocked. Light from outside streamed underneath the bottom edge.

"Please don't be anyone there," she whispered, unable to see outside. She had no idea what she was walking into.

Her mind kept flashing images of Ivar lying next to her in the vehicle as if she was supposed to remember something. Or was she just remembering him, that feeling she'd had while being next to him, the whisper of his breath against her cheek as they lay unmoving? Suddenly, finding him felt like the most important thing. What were they doing to him? What did they want with him? She had to find him. She had to save him.

With that goal in mind, she forced herself to open the door. She held it cracked for several seconds, listening for movement on the other side. No one shouted in warning at her escape, so she finally dared to look. A long row of small shacks spread out behind the house she was in like a tiny commune. Is that where the dragons lived? Is that where they were keeping Ivar?

Beth slowly stepped down the wooden steps to the back lawn. She kept to the shadows, hugging close to the cabin as she tried to catch her breath. The small shacks looked newly constructed. The aroma of fresh cut wood was strong as was the smell of the swamps wafting on the breeze.

There were too many shacks to search before being caught. She looked at each one she could see, trying to find movement in the small windows. There was nothing. She tried listening, but all she heard was the faint voices from the front lawn. Beth was sure her heart had never pounded so hard in her life. She inched to one side of the cabin, away from the voices, and peeked around the corner. A truck was parked close to the house, but it looked like it had seen better days. Apprehension filled her. Too bad she didn't know how to hotwire a vehicle. Even if she did, there was no telling if the old thing would even run.

"Are you safe?" Ivar's words whispered in her mind, the memory surely coming only to tease her with the past.

"Heck, no, I'm not safe," she muttered to herself.

She hurried to search inside the vehicle and pressed her face to the glass window. She was worried the old door might creak if she opened it. There were no keys in the ignition, so she rushed back to the cabin. Beth thought about running to the trees and going for help, but something stopped her. Ivar had to be here somewhere. If she ran, they might move him. If she ran, she might never find him again.

Beth didn't allow herself to succumb to fear though it would have been so easy in the given circumstance. No one knew where she was or that she was missing. Her job might report her gone, or they might have thought she was a no-show and didn't want to tell them she quit. Waitressing was a high turn over job.

Beth tried to make her way toward the nearest shack. She kept her eyes on the side lawn. A half constructed barn appeared from behind the corner of the house. In order to get to the shacks, she'd have to make a run for it and hope no one saw her.

Lori paced within her field of vision. Beth froze as the woman pointed toward the barn and ordered the men, "Now go back to work. The barracks aren't going to build themselves."

"Yes, ma'am," the dragons said. They moved toward the structure, looking more to the ground than at Lori as they went to do as she bid. Apparently, the lecture was over.

A few of them glanced up and saw Beth. She remained very still, holding her breath to see what they would do. Eyes flashed with gold, but after a small pause, they looked at Lori and then moved to go back to work building the barracks. The sound of hammering and saws soon inundated the quiet swamps.

Lori turned and stumbled a little when she saw Beth. "Oh, hey, good you're awake. How are you feeling? Can I get you something to eat?"

Beth looked around the yard. There was nowhere to run. She should have stayed hidden behind the cabin.

"Maybe I should start with, I'm sorry if they frightened you." Lori came closer as if scared Beth would make a run for it and she'd be forced to chase her down.

"Who are you people? Where am I?" Beth's voice sounded raw, and her dry throat ached.

"I'm Lori. This is my home. And those are the bayou lizard men." Lori gave a small smile. "But I think you know who they are, and I suspect you know exactly what is going on here."

"Where is the man I was with?" Beth

demanded. She wasn't sure where the false sense of bravado came from because in truth she was terrified.

"The cat-shifter?" Lori asked.

Beth nodded. She tried to relax when it appeared as if no one was coming to hurt her. Still, she didn't let down her guard. After all, she was kidnapped and being kept in the swamplands.

"So, you are with him? He wasn't chasing you?" Lori took another step forward. Beth matched the movement by taking a step back. She quickly darted her eyes around to make sure no one else was sneaking up on her.

Beth nodded again. "Yes, I'm with him. We were running from your men. You have no reason to hold us here. Let us go."

"The guys will be disappointed you're spoken for, but this explains why the prince was in New Orleans. He was there for you, not for us." Lori sighed. "That is a relief. My husband has been worried that the royals had located our whereabouts and were coming to force the defectors back to their home planet. And the fact you know all about it keeps me from having the very awkward conversation of," Lori's tone dropped into an almost bored sound as if she'd had said the words often, "these men are aliens, these men are dragon-shifter, these men won't eat you, please stop screaming."

"You're a dragon?" Beth looked the woman over for signs of shifting.

"No. I married one. His fate is mine. You know how it is to be mated."

Beth narrowed her eyes in confusion.

"You're not mated to the cat, are you?" Lori laughed. "A mated woman wouldn't look as you do now. Was I wrong? Do you have any clue what is going on?"

Beth didn't answer the pointed question. "Where is he?"

"I wasn't sure if the cat-shifter was a friend or chasing you, so I had them put him in one of the small houses." Lori motioned that Beth should follow her toward the shacks. "I thought you should have the more comfortable bed, being as you're human and may not have anything to do with what is happening here."

"What is this place?" Beth was slow to follow. She glanced around, keeping an eye on the trees and water. The construction noises continued.

"I told you. This is my home." Lori paused and looked at the barracks. "Did you ever see that musical Seven Brides for Seven Brothers where the woman gets married only to learn she suddenly has a bunch of brothers that she needs to domesticate? I'm the first wife, but instead of seven, I have seventeen new brothers, and they're all terrible with women."

Beth couldn't help the small laugh of disbelief that escaped her at the comment. She looked around the swamp compound.

"They can build a house," Lori motioned to the shacks, "but they get all crazy-eyed the moment a single girl walks by."

"Sounds like you have your hands full." Beth tried to keep her tone polite as she wondered which structure they kept Ivar in. "Why did they bring me here?"

"They were protecting themselves. They didn't know what else to do, and they didn't want to leave you in the alleyway."

"I was in the alleyway because they broke into my apartment. It was left wide open. Everything I own has probably been stolen by now."

"They told me they locked it for you," Lori said.

Well, that was something.

"I love my husband, and these men are his family. Maybe not actual brothers, but they need Drake's help and mine." Lori paused to clarify, "Drake's my husband."

Beth nodded not sure why the woman was telling her all this.

"These men are good people. They're hard workers and loyal, but they came here almost innocent. They know nothing of Earth life except some horror stories they were told about the medieval period when their ancestors left."

"So why did they come here if they're scared?" Beth asked, telling herself to be respectful. She needed this woman's help to get home.

Lori narrowed her gaze. It was the first aggressive gesture she'd shown. "I'll help you find Ivar, and if he is truly your man and means us no harm, then we won't have a problem. But there is no way I'm letting him take my family back to that awful place."

"I don't understand." Beth glanced at the houses. Which one held Ivar? How could she find him?

"That prince of yours. He is known to travel here with the dragon princes. Royalty sticks together. When cat-shifter nobles stole my husband's family's land, they asked the dragon-shifter leaders for help and were denied because of who was taking it. The royal families struck a deal, and Drake's family lost their property because the Myrddin clan noblemen claimed to have found old territorial documents that proved it was theirs. They could never provide the documents, but that didn't matter. It's the kind of primitive third world dictator shit that you hear about. I will never let them get taken back to Qurilixen against their will."

"I'm sorry, I don't know anything about what you're saying." Beth frowned. She'd been in shock since Ivar had told her of his home planet. There was so much she needed to come to terms with that the fact he was an alien had slipped her mind. Could it really be true? After all, she had her proof of shifters being real. Why not aliens? "Are they why rumors of the lizard men are hitting the Internet like crazy?"

"That would be Janice, the proprietor at the Plantation Inn," Lori said. "She thinks lizard men are good for business, like Area 51 and aliens. So she keeps posting nonsense about them, like how they're dangerous when provoked and eat alligators for breakfast. Then, drunken hunters come snooping around the swamps looking to cause trouble. It's why we are building our little village here. It's secluded, and there is safety in numbers."

"Why are you telling me this?" Beth wondered aloud. "If you think I'm with the prince, and the prince wants to take these men back to his," she stuttered over saying, "planet?"

"Because I'm hoping you will put in a good word

for us if and when the time comes," Lori said. "These men don't want to go home. They belong here now. There is nothing for them on Qurilixen. I don't know if the prince told you, but they don't have female children there. It's some genetic mishap. All they want is to live honorably, find a woman, settle down, have kids, and be happy."

"I feel for you," Beth said, "but I'm not sure there is anything I can do to help. I won't tell anyone if you're worried about that. As long as you let Ivar and I go, we can chalk this up to a misunderstanding. Now, if you don't mind, I need to see that Ivar is all right."

A splash sounded near the dock. Both women turned to watch a man jump out of the murky water. Brown armor covered his body, and his yellow reptilian eyes glowed. A protrusion distorted his forehead and formed a ridge of scaled tissue over his nose and brow. He wore the clothes of a man, well, the wet plaid pajama pants of a man. Ivar's fur had been soft. The dragons looked like they were covered in full body armor.

"Drake," Lori called, lifting her hand. "Come meet..." She looked at Beth expectantly.

"Beth Watson," Beth whispered, unable to keep from staring at the shifter.

"Meet Beth," Lori finished.

As the dragon-shifter strode toward them, his body morphed into that of a man. Somehow, the transformation from dragon to man was much scarier than when she had seen Ivar transform. His dark, wet hair did not change. Though handsome, he had a scar along his temple that added a dangerous vibe to his expression. Drake's yellow eyes did not appear welcoming. In fact, he studied Beth suspiciously as she if was a stranger trespassing on his land.

"Lena?" Lori asked.

"She is safe, *chere*," the dragon said, his voice deep.

Lori let go of a long sigh and nodded. "And Ursa? How is she?"

"She is much better," Drake said. "The sickness has left her chest. She breathes normally. I did as you suggested and informed her that there were new members to be made Cajun and that seemed to make her happy. She's willing to perform the ceremony for us whenever we are ready."

Drake eyed her again, and Beth felt the urge to back away from him. She needed to find Ivar. Even if that meant searching every single tiny house in this messed up village.

"Ursa is this crazy—" Lori began to explain.

Beth ran toward a shack. It wasn't the most logical choice. Nor was it the closest. But for some reason, she felt compelled to go to it. She had to find him. She had to know that he was safe. It was a need that burned inside of her.

Her shoulder met with the door, and she shoved her way into the small building. She expected there to be resistance. Instead, it opened freely, and she was flung by her own weight into the room. The space was tiny. A small bed looked like it doubled for a couch as it sat along one wall. An open door showed a narrow bathroom. A sink, stove, and dorm refrigerator made up the kitchenette area. The home was empty. She'd been so sure he was in there.

Beth spun around expecting to leave. A figure in the doorway stopped her. The man's hands were raised over his head as if he was about to strike. The breadth of his shoulders blocked the light from behind. She let out a small yelp of fright. Her arms lifted to block her face, preparing for the blow.

"Beth?" Ivar croaked her name, the word distorted and gruff.

Beth lowered her arms to her side. She took a deep breath. "Ivar?"

"Beth." Ivar dropped his hand, and she heard something clunk on the floor. "Are you injured? Did they do anything to you? How did you get here?" He wobbled slightly on his feet as if he was just now waking up from a drugged state. Having been in a similar situation only moments before, she understood how his mind might be muddled in confusion. "They did something to me."

"Take a deep breath." Beth reached for him. "It's going to be OK. Breathe."

"I was coming to find you. I swore I heard you say that you were not safe. Did they hurt you?" Ivar began to look her over as if studying her for injuries. His eyes glowed softly in the dim light, but they did not scare her like the dragon's had. Beth felt safe with him.

"No, I'm fine." She wanted to erase the worry from his expression. "But they are out there. We're in swamp country."

"I know that is not the truth. You are not fine. I saw what happened in the alley behind your home. They did something to you. I'm sorry I failed you. I should've protected you. Instead, I led them straight to your door. I should not have come into your home." He stepped back when she would touch him. "The gods were right to keep you from me. Just because I wanted you does not mean I deserve to have you. I am not worthy of a mate. I can't protect you. I have nothing to offer."

"Ivar what are you talking about? I think you are a little confused from the drugs they gave you to knock you out. Everything is going to be fine. They don't want to hurt us. They were scared that you were coming for them. I need you to go out there and tell them that they are free to stay here on Earth. Tell them you're not going to take them back to your home planet."

"I will do no such thing," Ivar denied her request. "I have every intention of making them go home. They do not belong here. They escaped through the portals without permission."

At that, Beth frowned. "I don't think you mean that."

"Yes. Of course I mean it. They left without permission."

Surely he didn't really believe that. It was so barbaric of a notion. "And who is the one to give them permission?"

"The Draig royal family. Dragons were not supposed to leave through the portals so soon. We were going to bring them to find brides when the time was right, and the plan was safe—after all four princes found wives to prove marriages would be blessed by the gods. It would be enough to calm fears and encourage men to travel through the right way. Now there are so many voices, all with an opinion and our plans are being threatened. On one side we have rumors of Earth being some kind of paradise and the royal family is blamed for keeping everyone from it. Then there are those fear mongers spreading rumors that dragon subjects are being sacrificed in order for the nobles to have women. Their leaving caused chaos."

"Ivar, you can't force people to stay somewhere they don't wish to stay." Beth wanted to make him see reason. "These people have chosen to be here."

"What is the sacrifice of a few when an entire world is at stake? Would you not sacrifice yourself to save your fellow humans? The fear they caused has spread through my world. People are demanding the portals be closed. Without the portals to Earth, we have no chance to marry, and no marriage means no children. Without women, our people die out in a few generations. We are out of options. It is why I came here with Prince Finn. We were going to marry anyone we could convince to prove that Earth was still a viable choice. If these men come back, it will let the others know that they were safe. They can teach others what they have learned. What they have done here is selfish."

"I don't think it's that simple, Ivar," she said.

"It is very clear," he argued. "The gods trapped me here so that I could find you and find them."

"These men are not going to agree to leave with you," Beth warned. "You're outnumbered."

"I am a prince. I will not give them a choice." He seemed so sure of himself.

Beth did not know what to make of this man. Something inside her felt connected to him, even if the words coming out of his mouth were not words she could agree with. To make somebody leave their home? To force them to sacrifice? It went against everything she was taught to stand for.

"Draig subjects need a firm hand, that is all. This would not have been happening if the portals were on Var land. Our guards would never have let men slip through. Portal travel would have been regulated, and this situation would not have occurred."

Beth frowned. "That seems a little extreme. How about we do not tell them that when they ask what your intentions are?"

"I will not lie."

"All right." Beth took a deep breath. He didn't seem to understand how dire their situation could become. "How about we tell the dragons that no decisions are being made today?"

"That would be correct. The decision to bring them home was already made before today."

"Great. Just don't mention that last part." Beth smiled. "And then they'll let us go."

Ivar shook his head. "I do not think so."

"Why? Don't tell them you're set on making them leave. It's not like we know how to get here. They can blindfold us and drive us to a bus station, and we'll never find our way back." Beth tried to keep her words calm, but it was hard to hide her apprehension.

"They already know."

"Know what?"

"My intentions. They're outside listening to what we say." Ivar gestured to the door.

"How do you know that?" she whispered. They weren't talking very loudly. She looked around for a listening device. The wooden walls were bare.

His eyes flashed. "Because I can hear them talking about it."

Beth pushed her way past him to go outside. Several men stood on the lawn staring at them. It didn't take a genius to see they had heard what Ivar said.

"We're not going back," Drake stated when Ivar joined her on the steps to the shack. "We are Cajun now. Not Draig. This is our home."

"Dimosthenis," Ivar stated. "You do not know what you started when you left."

"I am Drake of the Cajun now," Drake said. "Dimosthenis of the Draig is no more. Galen brought you so you could see that we have a life here."

"I'm sorry, Drake, I see that was poor judgment on my part," Galen said.

"You don't know what you have done." Ivar crossed his arms and faced the men on the lawn, not appearing worried by the fact he was outnumbered. "The elders are trying to close the portals forever. You will be trapped on Earth."

"This is my home," Drake answered. "It saddens me never to see the green skies or smell the sweet valley air of the Northern Mountains again, but we were left with no choice. Here we have a fighting chance at survival. We carve our destinies with our hands."

"And wives," one of the dragon men added. "Here they have women."

"All the things you royals deny us and keep for yourself," another put forth.

"Your brother and Prince Kyran both flaunted

their wives before us," another spat. "And you journey here whenever you wish, denying the rest of us the opportunity to be happy."

"Who are you to question our plan?" Ivar demanded. He crossed his arms over his chest. There was no fear in him, and that frightened Beth. "We know what is best for—"

"Uh, Ivar," Beth tried to interrupt. This didn't seem like the best way to ensure their freedom from the dragon-shifter compound. She was well aware of the eyes on them. The dragons moved closer. Inching forward as if they might attack at the slightest provocation. "Maybe you should tell them your plan for opening up the portals? You mentioned bringing everyone through to find brides when the time was right."

Beth really hoped he had a plan, and that it was a good one.

His eyes met hers. He began to lift his hand to touch her cheek but then hesitated. "You have fear in your eyes. Are you frightened of me?"

"Of course she's frightened of you," Lori answered for her. "Beth it's OK. You can come here. I promise no harm will come to you. We have no quarrel with you. It's clear you didn't know about any of this."

"Beth, I would never harm you," Ivar said, his tone softening.

There was something in his eyes that caused her to stay next to him on the stairs to the shack. "I know. I don't know how I know that. But I know. I think you need to tell the dragons your plan for the portal."

"If you think that is best." Ivar again turned to the growing mob on the lawn. The sound of construction stopped as more dragons joined them. "Staying on Earth is not an option."

"We do not wish to harm you. But you're not leaving us with many options." Drake stepped forward and angled his body in front of his wife to shield her.

"Var and Draig men will have access to the portal. All will be given a chance to find a bride. We had to make sure the portal stops were safe for our people. Already I have spoken to Prince Finn about establishing a celebration where men who are worthy are allowed to go through the portals to see if the gods will bless them. And, if they return with a bride, we will have a mass ceremony that will last throughout the entire night. We will build an embassy in the valley where both cats and dragons can gather."

"Who decides who's worthy or not?" a blond dragon in the back asked.

"There will be a system put into place. Those who have completed Earth training, and who have proven themselves honorable and able to care for a wife." Ivar stayed on the steps, looking as if he stood at a podium. There was a regal air about him, an arrogance that came with confidence. "Earth women are delicate. We all know—"

"No, they are strong and capable," one of the dragons interrupted. "Right Lori?"

"Yes, Pete," Lori answered, though she sounded distracted. "Now why don't you boys get back to work? We want to be ready if more show up, don't we?"

Most of the dragons went to resume their construction project. Galen and another man stayed behind with Drake.

"There will not be more," Ivar said. "The portals are under heavier guard now."

"Your guards cannot control the will of the gods," Galen said before turning to his friend for confirmation. "Gerard?"

"Those with the courage to leave will find a way through," Gerard agreed. His words were less accented than the others and easier to understand. "You can't stop us."

Beth held up her hands to stop what sounded like

a debate. "So what happens now? Can we agree to disagree and be on our way?"

"We can drive them far from here," Galen said.

"I don't think that's a good idea," Gerard said. "He knows about this place. They'll come looking for us."

"Drake?" Lori eyed Ivar in worry.

"They will be our guests," Drake said.

"You can't keep us here against our will." Beth leaned closer to Ivar and held his arm.

"You are free to walk out of here, but I wouldn't recommend it. We're deep in the swamps and," Drake held up his arm and let it shift with the hard armor of the dragon, "cat fur and human flesh is no match for an alligator's mouth if he gets ahold of you."

"Come on, Beth," Lori said. "You can stay in the main house."

Ivar placed his hand on Beth's shoulder. "She will remain with me."

Beth glanced up at him. Intuition told her to stay with him. She nodded. "I'll remain with Ivar."

"As my lady wishes," Drake said. "Rest if you like. Tonight we barbeque, and will speak more on this matter."

Ivar kept his hand on her shoulder as the others

departed. She took a deep breath, and whispered, "Can they hear us?"

He glanced around, waited a few seconds, and then shook his head in denial.

"What now? Do we run? Steal the truck? We can't stay here." Beth stayed close to him.

"They have offered us food and shelter. For now, we stay. Perhaps we can convince them to go home." Ivar's fingers caressed her arm.

"We?"

"Yes. Lori appears to listen to you. Perhaps you can get through to her about her husband." Ivar gestured that she should go back to the shack with him. "For now, let's rest. You are swaying on your feet."

"What about you?" Beth did feel tired.

"My head is not the clearest," he admitted.

Ivar held open the door. The shack was slightly cooler than outside, but at least the temperatures weren't too bad for this time of year. She went to the small fridge and was glad to find water bottles inside. She took one out and drank deeply, quenching the ache in her dry throat.

"You take the couch." Ivar pulled his shirt from over his head. "I will sleep on the floor."

Before she could answer, he was down on all fours and shifting into tiger form.

Beth eyed him as she lay on the couch. He paced the floor before settling next to her on a rug. His green eyes looked up at her.

"Sweet dreams," she whispered, not knowing what else to say to him. The things she felt swam inside her head, confusing her. There was just too much to process.

His answer was a soft growl and slight lift of his head. Beth closed her eyes, not resisting the pull of sleep.

11

IVAR DID NOT LET himself rest too deeply. His eyes closed, but he kept an ear on Beth's breathing. He was annoyed, but he wasn't angry at the dragon-shifters for taking him the way they did. He wasn't sure what they used here on Earth, but on his home world they would have knocked him out with a little of the yellow, a plant that grew in the Draig forest near the borderlands. To inhale it was to pass out. It was a common tactic, not used on princes necessarily, but used.

What did make him angry was the fact they took Beth in such a way. He could still see the stunned look on her face in the alleyway. She'd been so confused, so scared. She didn't deserve that. She'd only been trying to help him. The idea that he'd failed to protect her did not settle well in his stomach.

He felt a hand on his head and opened his eyes. She'd turned over on the small couch-bed in her sleep, and her hand had found his head. Her fingers twitched to stroke his fur as if in a dream. Every time she touched him, it was like a shock of electricity through his veins, and he wanted nothing more than to be worthy of her. At least shifted he didn't feel the burning desire to claim her. It was becoming harder and harder to resist. He stared at her face. She had lips that were meant to kiss him, and eyes that he could drown in.

Drowning eyes. He'd never understood that human phrase until he looked into hers.

The signs were clear. The gods were giving him a chance to prove himself. They showed him Beth and the dragons on the same night. There had to be a reason. To be worthy of Beth, he needed to convince the dragon-shifters to return home where they belonged. He needed to keep the portals open and save his people. If the dragons returned unharmed, that would help. It would prove the lost dragons did not die on Earth and that they chose to come home.

Ivar was not frightened by the shadowed marshes, or swamps as the locals called them, nor was he scared of these alligators that the Cajun tribe dragon leader warned him about. He had hunted yorkins. How bad could an alligator be?

Beth's fingers continued to stroke him, and he inhaled a deep breath, mesmerized by the contact. Her touch became more deliberate. Ivar's body tingled with awareness. He focused on that hand.

He hadn't realized just how lonely he had been on Earth. There had been no one to talk to, no physical contact aside from a couple handshakes and a fist fight. The sound of Beth's breathing, so soft and gentle, filled him as he listened to the rhythm of it. Her fingers touched flesh, and his shaft hardened in response. At some point, as he had lulled under the spell of her touch, he'd transformed back to man.

Ivar opened his eyes. He knelt on the floor, naked. When he looked up at her, sleepy eyes met his. Her fingers slipped onto his cheek, and she smiled. He was powerless. Everything about her invited him in, and he leaned forward to accept the invitation.

There was so much he wanted to say, but he couldn't form words. Their lips touched, and he felt his insides were about to explode. His heart beat hard and fast. He couldn't stop himself. The kiss deepened. Beth moaned, the sound an encouragement he could not deny.

His hand slipped onto her neck, and the delicate threads of her pulse thumped against his fingers. He could feel her excitement in the rapid beat. Her tongue slipped between his lips, and the kiss deepened even more. Her hands found their way into his hair. She pulled him close, urging him up from the floor.

Ivar was hers to command. He found his hands circling her waist as they dipped beneath her clothing to touch flesh. Time became meaningless. One moment she was looking at him with sleepy eyes. The next, he was pulling the shirt over her head. After that, her pants were gone, and he was touching her thighs. Everything he had been through was for this moment. This is where he was meant to be—in her arms.

He knelt before her. She sat up on the couch. Her naked legs parted, opening for him as she turned to face him. They brushed along both sides of his body. She wore lace over her chest, but instead of hiding her breasts from view, the material teased him with a peek at her nipples. They were hard, pressing forward to be free. He ran a thumb over the delicate peaks.

If the gods were tempting him with this as a test, he was going to fail. He could not deny her. Beth was his mate. He had no doubts. She was his. And he was hers to command. Anything she wanted he would give to her.

"I don't understand what's happening," Beth whispered as she gazed into his eyes. He saw her confusion, but more than that he understood her desire. It was as raw and hungry as his. She was not going to stop. "All I know is that I need it to happen. I feel you, Ivar. How can I feel you like this? For the life of me, I have no idea why I let you back into my apartment. I don't know why I tried to save you. I had to save you. When I woke up in the cabin, I should have run. Sane people would've run for their lives to get help. Logic didn't win. I could not leave you behind. I couldn't leave you now even if I wanted to. What is happening to me? Why do I feel like this? Who are you?"

"Do you not remember? My name is Prince Ivar of the Var. Humans have been calling me Ivar Othevar." He pulled back to study her face. Had she forgotten him already? He didn't understand. She seemed so clear in her intentions.

"I remember all of that. I meant why do I feel this way for you? All of my life I have never felt like this.

And I've dated some really nice men before. Not that I want to talk about other people right now while I'm naked, and you're naked, and we're kidnapped by dragons. But what I'm trying to say, why you? Why am I feeling this for you? I don't really know you. I just met you. Everything you say is insanity. This place is insanity. Dragon-shifters? Aliens? Princes? Cat-shifters? If you would've told me these things a week ago, I would've checked myself into a hospital." Beth took a deep breath. "Yet here I am. I'm staring into your eyes, and I want nothing more than to finish what we started. I was not looking for a relationship. Logic is telling me this is not supposed to be happening. But I want to kiss you. I want to keep kissing you. I want to understand what this feeling is. I want to know why I feel like I could fall in love with you."

"Beth, I—" Ivar started to say he loved her too, but she didn't let him speak.

"Is it a pheromone of some sort? Do you emit some kind of smell that makes women attracted to you? I hear animals can do that to other animals. It would make sense. Am I under some sort of pheromone spell? Is that it?"

"I do not have magical powers." Ivar didn't understand. She admitted to feeling so much for him, but at the same time doubted their connection.

"Oh, dammit, I'm so..." She panted for breath. Her skin was flushed.

Confused? Angry? Regretful? Ivar waited with held breath for her to end her sentence.

"Turned on," she finally finished.

Beth slipped off the couch and straddled his waist. She pushed back his shoulders. His arousal was thick with need, and she slid herself onto him. His shaft glided into her tight opening, and he gasped at the suddenness of her claim. She sat on him, pushing him inside. Her trembling breath caught, and she made the most alluringly delicate noise.

He pressed his forehead next to hers as she moved over him. Their eyes locked. The tension built and there was no fighting the climax as it rocked over them. He exploded inside of her.

"Wow." She almost looked stunned as she stared at him. "I'm not sure what came over me."

"We should not have done this. It was too soon. I was supposed to resist you." Ivar held her hips, keeping her on top of his lap as he sat back on his legs. It was not the most comfortable of positions, but he didn't care. He didn't want to have to let go.

"Is that your way of saying you regret what just happened?" Beth pushed at his shoulders, and he was forced to release her. She sat on the couch and began tugging on her clothes. Her eyes did not meet his.

Ivar wanted to pull her into his arms and hold her. He had not meant to upset her. But everything he said was true. He was not worthy of her yet. He was not strong enough to resist her. He was not strong enough to protect her. He had not accomplished the task the gods put before him.

"I regret..." He couldn't find the words.

"I see." She nodded, but the movement was strange and jerky. "I'm, ah, sorry I did what I did. No, that's not right. I'm *not* sorry I did what I did because I have no regrets. But I'm sorry that you're sorry about what we did. I have no excuse for my behavior. And I... I'm going to go see if the barbecue is ready."

"Yes, of course, you should go if you wish to help the other female cook." Ivar stood and moved out of her way. He didn't care that he was naked. There was so much that he wanted to say to her, but he could not form the right words.

"I'm going to pretend that you did not mean that comment to be as misogynistic as it came out." Beth shoved open the door and stormed out of the shack. When he tried to go after her, she made a low noise of anger and marched faster.

Ivar scratched the back of his head as he stood on

the stairs and watched her move across the lawn to the bigger house. A few of the dragons were on the grass watching him. One of them began to laugh. Ivar glanced down and realized that he was still naked.

"No need to be jealous, dragon," Ivar called, unashamed. He placed his hands on his hips and leaned his shoulders back. "It is not your fault you were not born with the manliness of a cat."

The dragon's eyes flashed, and his laughter died. Ivar sauntered back into the small building. His verbal victory was short-lived as his eyes went to the couch. He was not sure why Beth was so angry with him. He could only assume it was because she knew he was right. He had not proven himself worthy of her yet. But he would.

12

Beth looked anywhere but at her cat-shifter lover. He turned what should've been the most amazing, mind blowing, Earth shattering moment of her life into some regretful tawdry act. What man regretted having sex? That made absolutely no sense to her. They were both adults. They both wanted it. They both finished. What the hell was his problem?

Lori and her husband, along with her seventeen dragon-shifter "brothers," filled the long line of picnic tables that had been set up on the side lawn. Beth wasn't sure what she expected for the barbecue. However, seeing a bunch of alien shifters lining up for coleslaw, potato salad, and hamburgers off the grill was a little surreal. She held a hand over her mouth and tried not to laugh.

"What is so amusing?" Galen asked. The man sat across from her. He had been studying her as if he was searching for a secret.

"I was just thinking of an art critique I received the other day. A woman told me that I needed to go out into the world and find something to inspire my art. Now here I am in the swamps with aliens eating potato salad. I'm not sure this is what she meant." Beth lifted her fork and took a bite. Potato salad was not her favorite, but she felt obliged to eat it.

"You are an artist?" Galen prompted.

"I am." Beth nodded. She glanced at her favorite painting subject. Ivar held a hamburger and was sniffing it. Seeing her eyes on him, he set it down and returned her look.

"Beth is very talented," Ivar stated. His tone left no room for argument.

If the barbecue was an excuse to discuss the future of dragon-shifters on Earth, they weren't doing a very good job of getting the conversation started. No one seemed to be talking. Several of them stared at her in curiosity or observed Ivar with suspicion. There was tension. Flashes of gold flickered in the men's eyes. She saw peaks of dark armor shading the dragon-shifter's skin as if threatening to shift fully at the slightest provocation. Beth swore that she heard the threat of a growl in the back of Ivar's throat when he breathed. If someone didn't say something soon, Beth was worried that the gathering would erupt into a fight. And if that happened Ivar would be completely outnumbered.

"Who is this Ursa everyone keeps talking about?" Beth asked, in an attempt to break the silence.

"She is a powerful earth goddess," Galen said.

"She can transform us from Draig into Cajun with her swamp magic," Drake said.

"Swamp magic?" Beth looked at Lori, hoping she could translate. Instead, Lori kept her eyes on her plate and bit her lip to keep from laughing.

"She has performed the ceremony for all of us. We are Cajun now," Gerard said. Glancing down at the table, he mumbled, "Well, most of us. The rest of us will be soon."

"There's a magic ceremony to become Cajun?" Beth set her fork down interested in finding out more.

"Yes," Jerry nodded. "It is very sacred."

"Would you like to be Cajun?" Gerard asked.

"Can Ursa perform the ceremony on a woman?" Pete inquired.

"Ask them how Ursa does it," Lori advised Beth

before shoving her fork into her mouth. She proceeded to chew to hide her amusement.

Beth glanced around the table. All the dragon men looked so earnest. "How does she perform the ceremony?"

"First, you must drink from the special bottle," Pete said.

"The special bottle," Beth repeated, nodding.

"Then we are blessed by the swamp waters," Jerry put forth.

"OK. A blessing. Is that it?" Beth looked at Lori, not understanding what she found so funny.

"Ursa is like eighty years old. She gets them wasted on backwater moonshine, and then the guys swim naked in the swamp." Lori laughed.

"I don't know why you find swamp magic so funny," Galen said.

"I tried to stop it, but they insist," Lori added.

"And that is how we become Cajun," Jerry said.

Beth reached for a glass of water and began to take a drink.

"Would you like to be Cajun?" Gerard asked a second time. "I would be honored to come to your ceremony."

Beth coughed in surprise. Did Gerard really just

offer to get her drunk and watch her skinny-dip?
"No, thank you. I'm already a Louisianan."

Gerard's expression fell. "Oh."

Lori laughed harder. She didn't even try to hide it this time.

"I'm almost scared to ask," Beth said, "but you said another name earlier. "Lena? Does she perform the ceremony with Ursa?"

Lori's laughter stopped. She shared a long look with her husband before finally saying, "Lena Dimosthenis is our daughter."

"Oh? How old?" Beth asked. She found most people liked talking about their children.

Lori looked at her husband.

"She is two years," Drake answered.

"Oh, so a little one," Beth said. "Will we meet her?"

"She's staying at a friend's house for the time being," Lori said.

Beth nodded. "I understand. I probably would have done the same."

"You have kids, too?" Lori asked.

At that, Ivar gasped. Beth turned her attention toward him. He stared at her, his eyes rounded. "I did not know. You are not shackled to two men, are you?"

Beth shook her head. "No, not married." Then to Lori, she said, "And no kids."

"But you are mated," Ivar said.

"No. I said no," Beth answered. "Not married."

"But..." Ivar stood and pointed toward the shack. Instantly, several of the dragons dropped their dining utensils and also stood up from their seats. They looked at Ivar in warning. Ivar pointed at Beth. "We mated. You're my bride."

Beth's mouth opened, but no words came out. She had no idea how to answer. His bride? Was this his way of asking her to marry him? Her heart raced. At the same time, she became aware of all the eyes on them.

"You are mine," he stated.

Beth ran her hands through her hair and shook her head. "All of this is insane. I have tried to be a good sport. I have tried to go along with everything I've been told. And to tell you the truth I think I've done a pretty good job of not freaking out."

"You are not allowed to dictate claim of a woman," Pete stated. "She must be given a choice. Ask her."

"Stay out of this," Ivar said.

"I might be able to help," Lori offered. She walked around the table.

Beth held up her hand. "No, thank you. Ivar and I can discuss this later. I'd rather everyone addressed the elephant in the room."

"What is an elephant?" Ivar asked. "And which room is it in?"

"They are like a large ceffyl in size, but their faces are strange," Pete answered.

"Let's start with what everyone wants," Beth said. "Dragons want to stay. Ivar, you'd like them to go home."

"They must go back," Ivar insisted. "It is the reason why the gods stranded me here. That, and to find you."

"Aww," Lori sighed.

Beth glanced at the woman and arched a brow.

"What? It was sweet," Lori dismissed Beth's look with a small shrug.

"It is my duty to get you home," Ivar said. "I understand that you would like to stay. If it were up to me, I would let you. But this is bigger than all of us. I have a responsibility to the shifter people as a whole. I don't expect you to understand my position. As the oldest prince, when my parents die it will be up to me to fix things for cat-shifters, and to work with Prince Kyran to help the dragons. What would you have us say in four hundred years when the last of our kind is dying because there were no more female shifters born and we had no women to choose from because the portals were sealed shut? Should we tell them that once, long ago, there was a group of dragons who were selfish and left our world, caused a panic amongst the others, and we were forced to close the one option we had at saving us?"

"It is not fair to put all of that on us. We do not create controversy. We came here to be free to make our own choices," Gerard stated. "We will not be dictated to by royalty."

"Do you think I always get to make my own choices? Everything I do is dictated by my rank and my birthright."

"Let's not turn this into a who has it the worst contest," Beth interrupted. "Anyone can see the emotions run very deep on both sides of this debate."

"But how many chances must we give the princes to find brides until we're allowed to go?" Gerard demanded. "It is not our fault the gods have not chosen to bless them."

"Kyran and Rafe have succeeded in finding wives," Ivar defended. "And I—"

"Ah." Beth held up her hand. He stopped talking.

"Sadly, no children have been born, and there

has been worry, but now," Ivar looked at Drake, "you can show them—"

"Our child is not a prop," Lori broke in. All pleasantness left her.

"I do not think he meant to insult us," Drake assured his wife.

"I don't care. Our child will not be used for political propaganda." Lori glared at Ivar. "Go find some aliens to mate with."

"We tried," Ivar answered, not realizing Lori had meant it as a way of telling him to get lost. "The Draig do not associate with space travelers."

"It's true," Galen said. "The only reason aliens come to Qurilixen is because they want something."

"To push their religions," the blond dragon said.

"To steal ore from our mines," Pete added.

"Not all," Ivar defended. "There are just not enough of them that would be willing to stay on world. It's not like there is a bridal delivery service that would regularly drop off enough eligible women for us to choose from."

"What I don't understand, prince," Galen placed his hands on his hips, "is why did they send you to collect us? Were we not worth the time of a Draig royal?"

"Prince Finn and I were trying to keep the

portals open, and I was left behind when a portal closed," Ivar said. "I have been waiting for my opening to go home. However, finding you has been a top priority for both royal families. There are many people worried about you."

"Now you can tell them we're fine," Drake answered.

"It would be better if you told them," Ivar stated. "I believe the gods sent me here to bring you back."

"And I believe that the gods led us here to the bayou," Gerard said. "They gave us all the signs to find Drake and this place. It is where we are meant to be. On Qurilixen, I spent every day loyally working and taking care of the ceffyls in the royal stables. I did my job, did not cause trouble, kept to myself. When was I going to get the chance to come through? After the princes and nobles? After the guards? How many people would you consider more worthy of a wife before it was my turn? How many years until I had my chance?"

Ivar said nothing.

"As I thought," Gerard said, his tone mocking. "You can't answer."

"I can answer, but you might not like what I have to say," Ivar responded.

"I will not be going anywhere with you," Gerard said. "And if you try to take us, I will stop you."

A sound of agreement washed over the gathering.

"Go ahead and try," Gerard said.

"Are you threatening a prince?" Ivar asked with a growl. His eyes flashed in warning.

"I am simply stating a fact," Gerard answered. His brow hardened as the armored flesh of a dragon formed on his face. He began talking in a strange language. The words were gruff and fast. Ivar answered in kind. The men began to argue. The alien words were indecipherable.

"What are they saying?" Beth asked.

Both men glanced at her but kept talking.

Beth felt a hand on her arm. Lori tried to escort her away, but Beth pulled free.

"Trust me," Lori said. "You don't want to be in the range of their anger if it explodes."

"Then let's not let it explode," Beth countered. To the men, she said, "Surely fighting about—"

Gerard roared, leaping over the table at Ivar. He shifted mid-air before landing in front of the prince. Ivar dodged his taloned hand, rolling to the side. As he righted himself, he changed into the form of a man-cat. Both men stood on two legs as they faced each other. Dragons cheered, urging their friend on.

"They need to prove their point," Lori told Beth. "There is nothing we can do to stop it. They both need to show they are strong."

"This is barbaric," Beth answered.

"Yeah, it is," Lori agreed.

Gerard swung and missed, only to try a second time. Ivar dodged the blows and then swiped with his clawed hands as if testing Gerard's reflexes. The men danced around each other, growing bolder with each pass.

"Someone make them stop," Beth demanded. "Stop it!"

Ivar dropped his hands at her command.

Gerard lunged forward, taking advantage of the opening. His fist made contact with Ivar's face, sending him flying backward. The prince landed on his back.

Beth gasped, the sharp sound overly loud. "Ivar!"

Several of the men turned toward her.

Ivar looked at her, grinning. Beth didn't know what to think. Why in the world was he suddenly happy?

He growled, leaping from the ground. He slammed into Gerard's chest. The dragon crashed into the picnic table. Ivar didn't let up. He punched the man several times. Gerard managed to buck him off. He flipped back over the table and lifted his hands in surrender.

"She is spoken for," Gerard said. "I have said my piece about the dragons. We're not leaving."

Beth eyed the group in confusion. Spoken for?

Ivar grinned at her. A bruise formed on his cheek.

"You should probably go to him before another dragon tries to impress you," Lori said.

Beth walked to where Ivar stood. She gave him a stern look. "What was that all about?"

"I..." He glanced at the dragons.

"Tell her you will tame fifty yorkins for her," Jerry suggested.

"Tell her you like her ears," another dragon said.

"Ask her if she wants to saddle up and ride your big—" Pete began.

"Tell her she looks lovely," Lori interrupted.

"Ceffyl." Pete looked at Lori in confusion. "Women like to ride things. That man on the naked people show said so."

"Naked show?" Lori gave a loud sigh. "Did Sheriff Jackson give you guys movies again?"

"You look lovely," Ivar told Beth. "I don't think I ever said that. And you do have nice ears."

"What is going on?" Beth asked.

"Gerard offered to help me see if you were truly my mate," Ivar said. "He attacked me, and you were scared for me. So that means you love me."

"What? I..." Beth frowned at the men. "That is the most ridiculous plan I have ever heard. That proves nothing but that I didn't want to watch somebody get beat up."

"I have seen many movies," Gerard told Ivar. "I know how Earth relationships work."

"I will gladly tame fifteen—" Ivar began.

"Fifty," Jerry corrected.

"Fifty yorkins for you," Ivar amended his attempt at romance. "Although I am unsure why anybody would want a tame yorkin, let alone fifty of them. They are horrible creatures."

"You do know I can hear them telling you to say that, right?" Beth asked.

"It's romantic," Jerry said.

"That is very romantic," Drake agreed. "Would you like me to tame a yorkin, *chere*?"

"No," Lori stated. "Your Cajun butt is staying right here in the bayou."

"Yes, *chere*," Drake agreed.

The dragons kept talking. Beth pulled Ivar's arm and led him toward the shacks. When they were relatively alone, she said, "So are you fighting about everyone leaving, or about..." Beth gestured at Ivar and then herself.

"We are still discussing everyone's leaving," Ivar said. "I think I am making progress with them."

"You call that progress?" Beth shook her head. "I don't believe they like your plan to leave."

"They may not like it, but there are times when we must do what we do not like. The gods will reward those who live honorably." Ivar reached to brush a piece of hair off her cheek. His touch sent a shiver down her.

"So that black eye forming on your face was just a negotiation?"

Ivar smiled and gingerly tapped his fingers under his eyes to test the bruise he could not see. "No, this means you love me."

Beth was not sure what freaked her out more— the fact that he kept saying it, or the fact that when he said it, she believed it to be true. But how could she love him? Like everything else happening in her life right now, it made no logical sense.

A thought took hold in her mind. He said she loved him, but what about his feelings for her? He never said he loved her. In fact, he said he regretted being with her. Then he insisted that they were mated.

"There is something I never considered before," Beth said, studying him.

"What is that?"

"In my head, when you say alien and shifter, I automatically equate that to smart and powerful. It never actually occurred to me that aliens could have mental issues, just like humans." Beth shook her head and patted his arm. "I hope you get help on your planet when you get back."

Beth went to the picnic table and sat down in front of her plate. Lori gave a questioning look. Beth picked up her burger and took a bite. She nodded in appreciation of the meal as she swallowed. "Great food. Thank you."

13

IVAR WASN'T sure what had happened with his mate, or what he could do to make her happy. Reasoning with the dragons had not gone as he'd planned. Maybe that was the problem. He needed to try harder to convince them. But how? They made logical arguments and had sound reasons for wanting to stay. If it was true and the gods had lead them to the bayou, then why did the gods want Ivar to force them home? Was he supposed to beat them and drag them one by one into the portal?

He found himself walking the grounds. The swamps reminded him of the shadowed marshes at home but were still alien enough to make him homesick. It was evident the dragons were carving a life for themselves, accepting the Earth ways as their own.

Even the buildings they constructed lacked the look of a Qurilixen home. If he had to guess, he'd say the many shacks had been practice. They seemed to become progressively better going from one to the next.

It was different seeing the men living their lives than it was thinking about the defectors from the safety of his palace walls. These people did not look like criminals. They were only fighting for what they believed in—just as he would do.

He moved to the large structure they were building. It was as wide as the house but much longer. He touched the wood and studied the straight lines of the wall.

Drake joined him. Ivar had heard the man's approach but wasn't worried. If they were going to harm him, they would have never brought him here.

"You can try to push it over, but it's built to last." Drake nodded at Ivar's hand on the wood.

"Is this to be your palace?" Ivar asked. "Are you the new king of the Cajuns?"

"No, these are barracks. We don't have a king here. I would never presume to be royalty. The others look to me to lead because I was the first to come, and Lori has a way about her they respect, but I am no king. Seeing you, I can say I would never wish the burden on anyone." Drake moved to go inside the building. Ivar followed him. The skeleton walls created a large front room that led to a hallway. "We're building a place for shifters to live if they choose to come to Earth through the portals. Here they will be able to transition to the new world amongst the safety of friends."

Ivar looked around before staring at Drake. "Why are you telling me this? You know we will never allow more shifters to come through. We can't."

"I'm telling you because I have always heard you were a reasonable man, Prince Ivar. I am hoping that is true. Everyone knows that your brother is rebellious and wild. If it were Prince Rafe, I would not be having this conversation. People say you are stubborn, but that in the end you always do what is right. I believe the life we have here is right for us and blessed by the gods. I want you to see that. I want you to take that news home with you and convince the others to let us stay in peace." Drake walked out of the barracks. A small smile lifted his features as he looked around his home.

"I respect what you are trying to accomplish." Ivar searched the surrounding area for Beth, but couldn't see her.

"She's inside looking at photographs my wife took. It would seem we are both with artistic women," Drake said. When Ivar gave him a quizzical look, he laughed. "You're wondering how I knew what you were thinking, aren't you? I was newly mated once, too. Actually, I still look for my wife whenever she is not around. It's the way of things."

"I don't think Beth wants to be my wife. I feel her, but I don't understand her," Ivar admitted.

Drake laughed. "You may often not understand what she is doing, but that is a woman for you. All you have to do is honor and love her. Fate handles the rest."

"You know much about Earth women. This is my point. You should come back with me. Help us," Ivar said.

"We never meant for our leaving to cause problems for the rest of our people. We never wanted the portals closed. I can't leave my wife and child, but I will ask for a volunteer amongst the others to go with you. All I ask is you give me your word that whoever leaves with you will be given the option to return here."

"I give you my word that I will speak on the volunteer's behalf, but that decision will not be mine to make. The elders, as well as the kings and queens, have control over the portals. It is possible they will not agree to let the dragon return, ever." Ivar rubbed the back of his neck. His face ached where Gerard had punched him, but that was the least of his worries. "The Draig nobles were not pleased when all of you left. I don't think you understand how dangerous it has become. It's not the way it was when you left. My people hate feeling like we're at the mercy of the dragons and their decisions because the portal is on Draig land. Any decision the Draig royals make will be scrutinized. If dragons are allowed to return after defecting, it will create more chaos. If the cat-shifters protest, then dragons will argue that the Var need to recognize that they guarded the portals since our ancestors escaped Earth the first time. Draig took the risk that, if the human hunters ever found their way through, it was they who would be the first in their path. No decision we make comes without consequence, we are simply trying to choose the best path."

"I heard you were honest, too." Drake nodded. "Very well. I will ask the men, but I cannot promise one will return with you."

"Thank you, Drake of the Cajun. I must insist that you try to convince them. I fear a war is about to erupt between the shifters, and I am not sure my family can stop it." Ivar took a deep breath, hating the words but believing them to be true. He had a lot of time to contemplate the situation in his exile. "I can only imagine what my absence this last year has caused. Tensions must be running very high."

"Has it really become that bad?" Drake asked. "The new arrivals have hinted at things, but nothing on the scale you're talking about."

"We try to keep things quiet as not to incite panic. I don't know if you heard of the Nutef faction?" Ivar lowered his voice, not wanting any of the other shifters to overhear them. Drake nodded once. "They believe that taking human wives will dilute shifter blood and cause us to lose our natural abilities."

"That's ridiculous," Drake dismissed.

"I agree, but fear does not know reason," Ivar said. "The Nutef kidnapped my brother's wife and tried to kill her. They also took the Draig Princess Eve and brought her through the New Orleans portal to murder her on Earth. I heard rumors that they feared she might have been pregnant and wanted to hide any evidence that Earth women were compatible. We're not sure how they even knew where to find the portal. The valley entrance is kept locked, and the palace entrance is guarded. Someone had to help them."

Drake said nothing, merely listened.

"They will do anything to close the portals, including spreading the very rumors you cited as your reasons for leaving. It was never our intention to keep men out of the portals, but setting up safety measures takes time. We did not want to send men through without precautions. Then, when fear of human compatibility started, we found it necessary to lead by example. That is why we princes were to find mates first, to prove that it was safe. Sadly, there are no children from these unions, but by the will of the gods I hope that changes soon."

"I knew members of the Nutef had used the New Orleans portal, but I never knew about Princess Eve or your brother's wife." Drake's mood changed, and he paced several feet away to look up at the sky. After several breaths, he came back to where Ivar stood. "I believe you."

Ivar nodded.

"Montague," Drake stated as if it pained him to say the name.

"What?" Ivar frowned. "You mean Lord Montague the head of the Draig elder council?"

Drake nodded. "He allowed the Nutef through."

"How do you know?" Ivar asked, doubtful. Why would a Draig elder help a rebel band of cat-shifters? The Nutef were purists and Montague was, well, he was a complete elitist asshole to use the Earth term.

"Because he is the one who showed the others how to get here. He is the one who told us your plans to keep the commoners out of the portals." Drake frowned. "I never liked that man, but I did not suspect he would lie about something so important."

"I always wondered why they tried to kill Eve on Earth, but Jenna on Qurilixen. Montague must have been the one to tell them of Princess Eve's possible pregnancy and help them escape through the portal."

"Maybe that information will help you stop the war," Drake said. "If only the others could see this place as I do. No planet is perfect. Some humans do try to hunt the bayou lizard men, but for the most part, they believe us to be a myth. We can keep who we are a secret from humans. It's not perfect, but no life is."

"I need to get home." Ivar tried to see what Drake did in their surroundings. He supposed there was some beauty in the moss hanging from the trees. The landscape was much better than the concrete cities that blocked the view of nature.

"The New Orleans portal recently opened. It

won't be activated for many months," Drake said. "There is an entrance in Boston. Galen's brother might know when it appears. Though he said no one was using it."

Ivar felt relief wash over him. If the New Orleans portal had been opened recently, that meant the elders had not yet closed the portals. He would be going home.

"When Seanan disappeared and could not be recovered, they closed that portal out of fear it was an unsafe place. There was talk of strange weapons and, well, we know better now, but it was never marked as safe. I regret that fear has guided so many of our actions. Reopening a portal that was potentially deadly did not seem worth the political battle when we had so many other options, and it was never deemed necessary." Ivar shook his head. "Jenna came from Kansas City, but I never memorized when each portal would open where. So even if I was to travel around to the places I know..."

"The odds of a portal opening when you are in front of it would be very slim," Drake agreed.

"I have no choice but to wait for the Oxford portal to open." Ivar glanced to the shack where he woke up, "How many nights did I sleep before gaining consciousness?"

"Only the one," Drake said.

"The Oxford portal should open in sixteen days. I'll have to wait." Ivar felt the familiar frustration of his situation bubbling up inside of him. As much as he wanted to go home, he was also frightened by what he would find when the time came. Would the portal open? How would things look on the other side?

"Stay here," Drake said. "We'll get you to the portal on time."

"No. I can pick up one of the trucks I use for hauling supplies between Oxford and New Orleans. It will give me a chance to thank Toby for giving me work. He has been good to me." Ivar reached his hand out and held it in the air as he'd seen human's do to initiate a shake. "I will take Beth back with me. She will need to gather her belongings before we leave."

Drake took Ivar's hand, but instead of shaking it, he held it firmly. "You might want to watch how you handle that situation."

"What do you mean?"

"Ask her if she wants to leave with you before you assume that she does." Drake shook Ivar's hand once and released it. "If there's one piece of Earth knowledge I can pass onto you, it is that women do not like to be dictated to. They like to be asked. And they like to feel as if their opinions matter."

"Of course she'll come with me. She is my mate," Ivar said.

"Humans are not like shifters, prince." Drake chuckled as if at his own private joke. "They aren't born with the same innate sense of knowing that our kind has. They question more. Even when the truth of the situation is staring them in the face, they question it. It is in their nature. Just as it is in ours to know the second we look at them that we are to spend eternity at their side."

14

"Do you wish for me to take you home?" Ivar inquired as Beth approached him.

She was momentarily puzzled by his strange greeting but then nodded. "Yes. I would like to go home."

"Oh, not yet," Lori said. "Won't you stay longer?"

"I should be getting back to New Orleans. I need to see if I have a job waiting for me. No job, no rent, no house, no good."

Lori nodded. "I understand. Please know that you always have a place here in our sanctuary."

Lori left Beth alone with Ivar. The woman had given Beth some insight into what it was like to date a shifter man. They weren't like humans. Well, not like most humans, anyway. They carried with them some throwback traits from the Middle Ages from when they were last on Earth. Though they had a sense of honor and duty, they also had an infuriatingly alpha male quality.

He looked at the bandage Lori had wrapped around her hand. "Are you injured?"

"I cut it when we left the apartment. Lori bandaged it for me."

"You do not need a job in New Orleans," Ivar said. "There is no need."

Beth gave a small laugh. "You've been in this world long enough. I think you know how things work better than that. If I don't have a job, I don't eat, and I really like to eat."

"I will make sure you are fed," Ivar said the words like it solved every problem.

There was a part of her who wanted to see where this road led. How could she not be curious about the cat-shifter alien standing before her? There was an undeniable attraction. He may regret it, but it was there, burning as hot as ever.

But what kind of future did this path offer? A hard-headed alpha boyfriend telling her what to do? A trip through a portal to an alien world? She'd give up her art, her friends, her apartment, and her freedom. For what? A man who regretted sleeping with her and claimed they were married without bothering to ask her first.

The answer was clear.

"When do we leave?" Beth fanned her hands over her face. The evening was well upon them, but the air had become muggy.

"The portal opens in sixteen days."

Beth shook her head. "I meant, when do I get to go home to New Orleans?"

"Drake said someone can give us a ride tomorrow morning." Ivar looked over her shoulder. Dragons were bringing split wood to fire pits close to the docks and setting out camping chairs.

"Come on, let's join the party. Lori said she was going to roast marshmallows." At his arched brow, she added, "I take it you haven't been camping on your visit here. Here's one Earth tradition you should at least try before you go."

"What is a marshmallow?" He didn't move to join the others. "Will they fish them out of the shadowed marshes?"

"No. They are warm, gooey pieces of heaven shoved between graham crackers and chocolate." She threaded her arm into his. "Don't worry, I'll teach you how to do it."

At her touch, he nodded. He didn't resist as she

escorted him to join the others. Chairs were offered. They watched as dragons lit the campfires. Beth was a little disappointed that none of them started the fires with their breath. She thought all dragons breathed fire.

Ivar set five marshmallows on fire before he finally let Beth take over his stick to roast it for him. The sun set over the swamps, shadowing faces until they were orange glows in the darkness. Drake told the men of the conversation he had with Ivar, asking one of them to volunteer if they felt moved to do so. No one did. The men's words turned toward home, of green skies that only darkened one night a year. They spoke of three suns, and valleys that smelled like spun sugar. Their horses were called ceffyls and looked like a reptilian mated with an elephant.

As much as Beth wanted to relax, she couldn't help remembering how they'd broken into her home and brought them to the swamps. Yes, they had their reasons, but that didn't change the facts.

Stories were told of boys causing mischief in the forests, hiding in trees from their parents, fighting over forgotten incidents, shifting forms freely and without worry of being seen. They had grown up wild, running the countryside without cell phones or GPS. The picture they painted was so vivid, so beautiful, that she wondered how they could have ever left it.

"And you don't want to go back?" she asked.

Eyes turned to her at the words. Some were sad, others nostalgic, and still others were defiant. There was much emotion wrapped up in the answers to her question.

"It is our past," Galen answered when no one else did. "This is our future."

"So, what happened?" Beth asked. "Why are there no more females to marry? Did they all leave with alien visitors?"

"Female shifters are no longer being born, and haven't been for over a generation," Ivar said.

"Why? What happened?" she asked.

"We're not sure. Some say the will of the gods," Gerard answered.

"Bad luck," Galen offered.

"Our scientists think it might be the radiation that comes from our three suns. They believe the blue sun altered us somehow. It's made us stronger, but it took away our ability to have female children. It has been estimated our people will die out within a few generations if we do not fix the problem." Ivar lifted his hand to take hers.

"I have decided," Gerard stood. "I will go with

you back to Qurilixen. I will tell them Earth is a safe enough place."

Beth gasped. Out of all the dragons, she would not have guessed Gerard to be the one to volunteer.

"Thank you," Ivar said.

"We left to forge a new life, not to condemn our old one." Gerard sighed and walked toward the swamps. His shoulders slumped, and Beth realized he did not want to leave his new home. He was leaving because they all believed someone had to. "I will be ready to go in the morning."

"I can drive everyone to New Orleans tomorrow," Galen said. "Then I will go up to Boston to see my brother."

Beth looked at Ivar's fingers stroking the back of her hand. His touch sent a tiny shock wave of desire through her. It made sense now. He wanted a woman to take back with him to help repopulate his planet. He had hinted as much in different ways. She was a means to an end, the reason he'd come here. He didn't love her.

Attraction was not love. That must have been what he meant when he said he regretted it. He regretted having to choose a woman he did not love as his wife. He came from a society where apparently males were used to making the decisions. Some medieval world where it never occurred to him that she would say no.

Beth was not some medieval maiden used to taking orders. She was saying no. She was saying no to a life without love. She was saying no to being used as a political pawn to stop a portal from closing. She was saying no to Ivar. She did not want aliens she had never met to die. But from everything she had heard she wasn't sure that keeping the portals open would save them. Beyond that, she wasn't sure that her going with Ivar to his home planet would keep them open. It sounded like a hot mess of politics and age-old rivalries.

For some unknown reason, Maura Masters' words filled her. The woman had told her that she needed to take chances. She said Beth needed to go out into the world and feel something and fuel her art with it.

When Beth looked at Ivar, she felt something. It was profound and beautiful and painful all at the same time. He was filled with honor, a duty that made him want to save his world. There was a piece of her that never wanted to leave him that wanted to go with him and help him in his heroic journey.

There another part of her that knew she could not leave with him. They were not meant to be.

He did not love her. If she stayed with him, she would fall in love with him, and that was begging for heartbreak.

This wasn't some romantic movie where everybody rode off into the sunset, or in this case through a portal opening to another planet, to live happily ever after. No, this was reality. What happened when reality took hold? After a month, or a year, or two years when she looked at him and realized he couldn't care for her the way she cared for him? What happened when she stood in the forest and saw three suns over her head and began to feel homesick? What happened when they expected her to be a princess and took away her paints and her paintbrushes? Beth had no proof that would happen, but she also had no evidence that it would not. Her art was her life. She worked so hard to make it happen. Maybe this heartache she felt was the fuel she needed to take her work to the next level.

The shifters kept talking about the will of the gods and fate. They argued about it. The choices Beth made now would decide her destiny.

"I'm exhausted," Beth pulled her hand out from under Ivar's. She nodded in the general direction of the dragons and smiled at Lori. When Ivar stared up at her, she tilted her head that he should come with her. He eagerly stood, said some gruffly worded things to the rest of the gathering, and hurried to escort her back to the shack they shared.

Beth didn't speak as they went inside. Ivar shut the door, and she instantly moved into his arms. Her lips met his, testing to see if he felt what she did. The desire between them couldn't be questioned, even with his regrets. It was there, hot and burning, and it pulled her to him like two souls being sewn together.

She felt a sadness knowing that their time would be so short. Soon he would be going home, and she would have to say goodbye. Their kiss deepened, and all thoughts left her.

Hands roamed over flesh. Lips met and parted only to meet again. Clothing fell to the floor. Moonlight came in through the window, but it was barely enough to see by. Ivar laid her down gently on the couch. They made love slowly, caught up in a web of passion. With each thrust, Beth felt their connection growing. They came at the same time, and Beth cried out softly.

He settled next to her, holding her in his arms. Ivar opened his mouth to speak.

Beth pressed her fingers to his lips to stop him. "Shh, don't say anything."

If he dared to say he regretted what they did, she couldn't be held accountable for her reaction.

Ivar nodded and said nothing. He stroked her hair back from her face and kissed her temple before closing his eyes. A small smile formed on his lips. Beth lay awake, staring at him, memorizing the lines of his face. She never wanted to forget a single detail.

15

IT WAS impossible to talk about anything personal while Galen drove them to New Orleans. They left before dawn, probably to help hide the location of the dragon compound. The SUV was an older model and ran a little loud. Galen tried to make conversation. It didn't work. Gerard was quiet, staring out of the passenger side window. Beth sat in the back seat with Ivar. She tried to doze, but the bumpy back roads kept jarring her awake.

Before they went, Lori handed Beth her phone number and invited her to return. She also gave her a stack of envelopes with photographs and letters to send back through the portal, saying, "I don't know if it will help, but maybe if Ivar's people see the dragons are happy here it will calm their fears." Beth peeked at one of the letters but could not read the language it was written in. The photos were of Drake, Lori, and their daughter, as well as several of the men.

"Look." Beth pointed out the window as they drove past a cemetery. "Vultures."

"The birds?" Ivar asked.

Beth nodded. "They're scavengers. I don't usually see them in this part of town."

"Perhaps it is a bad omen," Gerard said.

Galen slowed the car for a few seconds to look at the birds before regaining his speed.

Beth gave Galen directions toward her apartment. Ivar's hand rested on her knee. The warmth of his fingers brushed her leg. She still wore her lucky white skirt. Even though she'd showered at Lori's, she still wanted a change of clothes.

"We should do some things before your portal opens," Beth offered. "I would hate for you not to have some fond memories of Earth. What kinds of things do you like to do?"

"Run in the forest," Ivar answered. "Hunt yorkin and baldric."

"You should try roasted chicken with creole seasoning," Gerard said. "Tastes like baldric."

"All right, you like outdoorsy stuff," Beth

concluded. Though looking at his physique, she couldn't say she was too surprised by that. "I'm not taking you hunting because I couldn't shoot at anything, but maybe hiking? We could find some nature trails." She looked out of the window trying to come up with suggestions. "We have some haunted bed and breakfasts. We could hunt ghosts."

"What are ghosts?" Ivar asked.

"The spirits of people who died that are said to be trapped on this earthly plane," Beth said.

"You hunt your dead?" Ivar grimaced in disapproval.

Galen shook his head. "I know nothing about this."

"OK, bad idea," Beth quickly dismissed. "Forget I said anything about ghosts."

"Hunting is not the same here," Gerard said. "You cannot shift."

"Is there anything else you enjoy doing?" Beth asked.

Ivar's eyes met hers. "There is little time for anything beyond duty."

"Oh." She looked at her hands in her lap.

"I'm turning, where to next?" Galen asked.

"Two blocks up and then go right. We're almost

there." Beth turned her attention back to Ivar. "Was there nothing about your visit to Earth you enjoyed?"

"I like gladiators," Ivar said.

"Gladiators?" Beth instantly thought of the Roman Empire and men being forced to fight to the death.

"Yes, you call it football." Ivar nodded. "I enjoyed your football. I went to the Oxford footballing stadium and drank beer and carried around a corn dog from the valley of tents. I'm not sure why I carried the corn dog, but I fed a kid with it."

"Fed a kid?" Beth frowned.

"Yes, he ran by, grabbed it in his mouth, and took it with him," Ivar said.

"I like the basket battles," Galen put forth. "I do not understand what they are fighting over, but I enjoy it."

"Basket battles?" Beth met his eyes through the rearview mirror. "Do you mean basketball?"

"Yes. They are excellent warriors," Galen said.

"I will miss sports," Gerard inserted softly.

"It is hard to believe I will see my home again in fifteen days," Ivar caressed Beth's cheek.

"When I left, I thought it was for good." Gerard's expression carried sadness whenever he talked about leaving as if he'd just seen all his dreams shattered on the ground around him. He'd lost hope. He came through the portal looking for a wife and was going home alone.

"I thought I would only be gone for a few hours," Ivar admitted. "My trip was not supposed to last for three hundred and sixty-five days."

"You mean three hundred and fifty days," Gerard corrected.

Ivar frowned. "No, I mean a year. The portals open once a year."

"Roughly once a year," Galen said, "but taking into account Earth calculations, it's three hundred and fifty days, about two weeks short of the Earth year they put on the calendar. We never go by their twelve-month system when it comes to calculating travel."

Ivar leaned forward in his seat and looked as if he was tallying days in his head.

"You didn't know?" Gerard asked. "So, when you said we had fifteen days…"

"Tonight," Ivar whispered, reaching forward to grab the back of Gerard's seat. "We have to get back to the portal, or it will close for another year."

Beth saw his panic and placed a comforting hand on his leg. "It's all right. Oxford is only about five or six hours from where we're at. We can still make it. If we stop by my apartment, I will grab a change of clothes and cash for road snacks. We'll be there by nightfall."

Ivar took a deep breath and nodded. "Yes. Very well. We will do as you suggest."

Nightfall.

Beth tried not to think about it. This wasn't fair. She was supposed to have two more weeks with him. She wasn't ready to say goodbye yet. The ride became as quiet as when it had started.

They reached her apartment, and it took some searching to find her keys. The last time she had seen them was in the alley as they escaped out of the window to get to her car.

"I apologize we took you the way we did," Gerard said.

"As do I," Galen added.

Beth nodded. "Thank you for saying so."

The car was still parked where she'd left it. She was lucky it hadn't been stolen. They were able to find her keys next to the building under the metal stairs.

The men waited outside as she went to her home. The dragons had locked the door, but they hadn't picked up the mess. Beth started to straighten the apartment, only to stop. Now was not the time. She changed out of her clothes, leaving her lucky skirt in the hamper. Jeans and a long sleeve t-shirt seemed much more practical for the drive. She packed a change of clothes and grabbed what cash she had on hand from her last waitressing shift. She took her camera bag and started to leave, only to stop. Going back to her paintings she grabbed her favorite portrait of Ivar. When he left, she'd want him to take it with him to remember her by. She wrote a note to Yvonne telling her not to worry, that she would be home soon, that the woman could borrow her car again if she needed it since she already had a key to Beth's apartment, and that she was going to Oxford with the painting muse. She also mentioned not to worry about the party mess in the apartment, so the woman wouldn't panic when she saw it. The woman would get a kick out of Beth having a party and going away with a sexy man. She slid the note under Yvonne's door.

"Do you have everything you need for the trip?" Ivar asked, rushing forward to take her bags and the painting.

"Yes." Beth nodded, giving him everything but the camera.

"It is good you packed light," Ivar said as he

opened the SUV door for her. "I will be able to provide anything you need."

"Ivar," Beth touched his arm. She glanced at the two men and waited as they climbed into the vehicle. She shut the door without getting inside. She didn't want to be overheard. "I can't leave with you. This is my home."

He stared at her mouth as if trying to understand what she was saying.

"I sympathize with your plight," she continued, "and as interesting as it would be to know I'd been to another planet, it doesn't sound like a trip I should take. We only just met. I like you, and I wanted to spend the next two weeks with you, but..."

His lips pressed tightly together, and it looked as if he didn't breathe.

"I know you're disappointed. I'm sorry for that. I will help you get home, and you know where I live. If you make it through the New Orleans portal, come over and say hello." Beth tried to touch him, and he inhaled sharply. She dropped her hand. His eyes seemed to ask why, but he didn't speak. "I cannot be a figurehead wife, a princess no less, on an alien world. You don't even know for sure if the portal will remain open if you were to bring a mate home. I could go, and it might not even work."

Her words caused her pain, and she felt an intense loss when saying them, but what else could she do? If she went, and they didn't work out, she could be trapped on an alien planet she knew nothing about. Did they have artists? Did they have restaurants she could waitress in? How would she survive? Then there was the fact that it was a male populated world. What kind of rights did a woman have in such a society? There were too many questions, and more she was sure she hadn't even thought about.

"You... don't..." His words trailed off as if he couldn't form the thought. She patted his chest, fighting the tears that tried to form. Slowly he nodded, standing very still.

Beth reached to open her car door. "We should get on the road."

"As you wish," he whispered, walking around the SUV to climb inside.

16

IVAR HAD THOUGHT he knew all the times he had felt real fear. First, when he witnessed that spaceship appear like a ring of fire to land on top of his palace home. Second, when scientists admitted that there was no solution to the shifter reproduction problem. Third, when Jenna had been taken to be sacrificed by the Nutef faction. And finally the night he was locked out of the portal and exiled to Earth for a year.

He had been wrong.

None of those things constituted real fear. They were nothing compared to the heartbreak and loneliness he was feeling on the journey to Oxford. Beth did not want to come with him.

He couldn't move, could barely breathe. He felt her looking at him from her place next to him on the seat. He couldn't meet her gaze. If he looked at her, he knew he would be tempted to force her to leave with him. How could he do that to her? If he took her, it would be selfish. She wanted to stay. And if he loved her, he needed to let her stay.

So he sat for hours, unmoving and broken. The stiffness in his muscles became uncomfortable, but what did that matter? It took all his concentration to keep breathing with the pain in his chest.

The landscapes were lost on him, blurred trees and pastures that did not stay in his thoughts. They stopped for fuel and food. Ivar could not bring himself to eat. The dragons spoke, but he had no presence of mind to answer them. Beth touched his hand, and the pain worsened, but he didn't pull away from her. He would take the agony of her touch for as long as she gave it.

Ivar considered staying on Earth. So what if he did not enjoy living on the planet? He could learn to like it. He liked football. He loved Beth. He liked the dragon-shifter colony. He could learn to be happy. For a moment, he let himself fantasize about what it would be like. Sadly each fantasy left him feeling more hopeless. What kind of life could he provide for Beth? He had no earthly skills. It was not as if they were hiring princes. He could drive a truck back-and-forth from Oxford to New Orleans. He could not provide for her in the way that she deserved. But maybe he could try. He was willing to give her everything he had. He wanted to treat Beth like a princess.

But what about his people? His parents? His duty to all of them?

Oxford came too soon, and he did not have the answers. His chest tightened with each mile. The familiar streets felt like they were closing in on him.

"Lori wanted you to take these photographs with you. She thought it might help show your people how happy the dragons are." Beth slid an envelope onto his lap. "There are also some letters from the others."

Ivar managed a nod. His eyes met hers, and he felt helpless.

"I also want you to take the painting I did. I know it's not much, but I want you to have it." Beth motioned to the back where he had placed the portrait next to her travel bag.

He again nodded.

"For the last five hours, I have tried to figure out what to say to you. I'm sorry you're upset by my stay-ing." Beth's hand trembled against his. "I wish we had more time."

At the comment, Gerard sighed heavily and nodded in agreement.

"I have given it much thought," Ivar stated. "I will return home alone."

At that Gerard twisted around in his seat to stare at him. "What do you mean? I thought you said you needed one of the dragons that had come to this world to go back with you to prove Earth was a safe place. What has changed?"

"I have had time to consider," Ivar said, unsure how he managed to form the words. "It is not fair to ask you to give up your chance at happiness. You have proven yourself honorable in your willingness to come with me. These photographs will have to be enough evidence. As it has been said, there is no guarantee any of my suggestions will stop the portals from closing. But, since the dragons were able to come through recently, I will be able to go home and try. I will tell them of your success here. My word will have to be enough."

"Thank you, Prince Ivar, thank you," Gerard said, smiling.

Ivar could not return the happy expression.

They parked downtown in Oxford and climbed out of the car. Ivar went to Galen and held out his hand in the Earth shaking custom. "Please watch out for her. Anything she needs."

Galen nodded. "I swear on my life."

"You should stay hidden when the others arrive," Ivar said. "Wait for the portal to close before you leave. I will explain your situation once I'm back on Qurilixen."

Gerard and Galen both nodded. Beth came around the side of the car holding her camera bag. The camera was in her hands. She lifted it and motioned for the men to stand together. When she lowered it, her eyes met Ivar's and she bit her lip in uncertainty.

"I will take you back to your home before I go to Boston," Galen told Beth. "We will not leave you stranded here."

Ivar took Beth's hand and led her away from the dragons. He walked the familiar sidewalks to where his statue friend sat. "We will be able to see the portal opening from here. It should not be long now."

"You've been quiet today," Beth observed. "Are you excited to return home?"

"Not as much as I thought I would have been." It was the truth. Every other happiness in his life paled next to the pain of what was to come.

"Do you think you will visit me through the New Orleans portal?" Beth asked.

"I will do everything in my power to try," he said.

Now he had even more motivation to keep the portals open. This wasn't what he wanted, but he'd take it. Seeing her for a few hours, once every three hundred and fifty Earth days, was better than nothing. Perhaps in time, she would change her mind.

"I have spoken with Galen. I would like you to keep in touch with the dragon-shifters. They will keep you safe," Ivar said.

"Safe from what?" Beth frowned.

"From everything," Ivar said. "I will not be here to look after you."

"Ivar, I have been looking after myself for many years now. I don't suddenly need a babysitter." She leaned forward and ran her hands through her hair. "I really wish we had those two weeks. I feel like I was just getting to know you."

"I feel like I already know you." Ivar couldn't stop himself. He wrapped his arms around her and held her close.

Everything that he wanted to say would not be fair to her. He wanted to beg her to come. But she had made up her mind and was very clear about it.

Beth held him tighter. "Where will the portal be?"

Ivar pointed toward Faulkner Alley. "There, beside a black door with a skull."

"The grilled cheese place?" Beth asked.

"No, a black door with a skull," Ivar corrected.

They both stared at the opening to the passage-way. Suddenly a soft purple glow shone from within. It only lasted a few seconds. Ivar stiffened and pulled her closer. He did not want to let go. He did not want to leave her. He again thought about staying on Earth.

"Is that...?" she whispered. Her hands kneaded against his chest.

Ivar nodded. "Yes."

"We should go to the car and get your painting," she said, her words hesitant.

"Yes."

"Maybe we should get you some food for the trip? Will it take long?" Beth made no move to leave the bench. She held him tighter.

"That light means somebody came through. They are probably looking for me," Ivar stated. He slowly stood, forcing her to move with him. He glanced at the statue but felt no need to speak to it, not like before. He had Beth to talk to now, and he wanted to take every second he could.

"What would happen if you stayed?" Beth asked. "Maybe you can tell them that you're well. And they could go home and let the others know you're safe here. Could you use a New Orleans portal to get home later, or I can bring you back in a year?"

"Are you asking me to stay?" Ivar touched her cheek. Her request restored some of his happiness, and the ache in his chest lessened.

Beth nodded. Her eyes searched his. "If you want."

"I have to go home," he said. "I need to know what is happening on my planet. I need to make sure the people see me, and my absence is explained."

He also needed to tell the Draig royals about Lord Montague's part in the unauthorized portal travel. Since the old house noble was well respected amongst his peers, it would take some very delicate political maneuvering to expose him as the traitor he was. There were those who would not want to take the word of the deserters against the leader of the elders.

Ivar wanted to stay. Duty demanded he go.

"Are those...?" Beth blinked, pointing toward the portal opening.

Ivar turned, expecting to see his brother and Prince Finn coming for him. It was easy to detect the two men who did not belong on this world. One wore the cross-laces of the Var, the other the looser tunic style of the Draig. Ivar wondered if he had looked so out of place when he came through.

"They must be here for me," Ivar said. "I expected my brother, at the very least, or Finn. Something must have happened."

A warning sensation worked its way over him. Something felt off. There was no way his brother would not be here. If it had been Rafe abandoned on a planet, there was no way Ivar wouldn't go after him.

"Do you have to leave right this moment?" Beth asked. "I feel like we should…"

There was so much he wanted to say. He felt like he did not have enough time, so the words came out in a rush, "Beth, if my life were my own I would give up my world for you. I would stay here on Earth and figure out a way to be the man you deserve. Never before in my life have I wished that I were not a prince. I have always accepted my place and never resented my role for my people. But never have I had to give up a woman like you. It is tempting. Please know that I want nothing more than to turn around and forget the portal even exists." He touched her face. "I do not know these men. It would be best if you stayed back. I do not want them thinking they have to push you through the portal because you know the truth."

He saw the men looking around and pointing. It was only a matter of time before they found him. They would sense another shifter was close, just as Ivar sensed them.

"Ivar..." She grabbed hold of his arm to stop him from leaving.

"I love you, Beth. There will never be another for me. Only you." Ivar kissed her and then set her away from him. "Be safe. Don't follow me."

She gasped, touching her lips. "But..."

He left her beside his favorite statue. The men found him almost instantly, and he walked quickly toward them.

"Prince Ivar," the cat-shifter said. "It's good to see you unharmed. Come. We have been sent to escort you home."

"Where is my brother? Did Prince Finn make it through the portal all right? What about the woman that went in after him?"

"Princess Sadie? Yes, she and Prince Finn both

made the journey," the dragon-shifter said. "They are waiting for you on the other side, in the caves."

"Sadie," Ivar nodded. The guilt he felt about pushing the woman through that first night lessened. It would seem the gods wanted him to send her to her future. He glanced back to look for Beth. She'd moved from the bench and now stood across the street watching him from behind a sidewalk railing. Her fingers lifted as if to wave. He gave a slight nod and turned back to the men, hoping they didn't see the interaction.

"Are you waiting for someone?" the dragon asked.

"Who are you?" Ivar didn't make a move to leave, but he did step to the side as if he might soon. He drew their attention away from where Beth stood, forcing their eyes to follow him.

"We are palace guards," the dragon said. "I am Hackett."

Ivar turned to the cat. He knew all the Var palace guards, but he did not know this one. He'd trained and spoken to every single one of them. "And you?"

"Tavas," the cat-shifter said.

"You must be loyal servants if the kings and queens sent you to me." Ivar glanced around, noticing just how many humans were in the area. He did not wish to cause a scene.

"Yes," Tavas said. "My family has served your family for generations."

"My parents were farmers," Hackett said. "I'm the only one in my family to leave the trade. Six of us brothers and I am the only one who does not like to shove my hands in the dirt."

Tavas chuckled as if they shared some great brotherhood bond in their positions.

Ivar nodded. "I am ready. Lead the way."

The men walked ahead of him. He turned, seeing Beth starting to come after him. He held up his hand, motioning her to stop. They went inside the narrow passageway of Faulkner Alley.

"There are many people worried about you." Hackett glanced back to make sure the prince was still following them.

Ivar didn't answer. A third man waited for them. Ivar narrowed his gaze, letting his vision shift with the power of the cat to pick apart the shadows. A dark cloak wrapped the man's shoulders. Thin lines were cut like rivers from his eyes, signifying his age. The cold look in his gaze was sinister.

"Lord Montague," Ivar stated. "What are you doing here?"

"I volunteered to escort you back," the dragon elder said.

"You hate Earth," Ivar countered. "You have said so on many occasions."

"It is true," Montague glanced around in disgust. "I do hate this planet."

Ivar's senses prickled. He knew when something was off. Drake had told him about Montague's connection to the Nutef faction. Tavas lied about being a palace guard. Even if Ivar had not trained the men himself, this man did not carry himself like a Var soldier.

It was a trap. Who knew what awaited him on the other side. Tavas came a little too close to him.

Ivar balled his hand into a fist. He roared, throwing a punch to knock the fake cat-shifter guard back. Tavas flailed in surprise. He hit the wall near the portal. His hand dipped inside, activating it for a second before he pulled back out.

"Grab him! We need him," Montague ordered. "Without him, we have no leverage against the royal families."

Ivar turned his attention to Hackett. Claws extended, he slashed at the man's face, drawing blood before the man shifted into dragon form. Ivar slammed him against the wall, knocking his head hard. The dragon growled in outrage.

Claws hit Ivar's back, slashing through his flesh. The narrow passageway made it hard to maneuver. He flung back his elbow, making contact with a chest. He kicked the dragon, landing his foot in Hackett's stomach.

"I have to do everything," Montague grumbled. He surged forward, talons drawn and eyes glowing with deadly intent as he slipped his arm over Ivar's neck and squeezed. Ivar clawed at the man's armored flesh, but Montague held on tightly.

He kicked at Hackett when the man would get up to help Montague.

"Ivar!"

Beth's voice brought him back from the edge of passing out. The sound of running feet reverberated in the passageway. There was a thud, and Montague's body jarred and his hold loosened. Ivar took hold of the elder's arm and flipped him. Montague whipped over Ivar's shoulder and slammed down onto the pavement.

Beth screamed as Tavas grabbed hold of her. She dropped the broken piece of wood she held in her hands.

Ivar slashed at the man's neck, ripping flesh

before throwing him into the portal. Tavas disappeared. Hackett moaned. He must have fallen to the ground after Ivar's last kick. He tried to stand. Beth kneed Hackett in the jaw to keep him down. The blow knocked the dragon-shifter unconscious. She breathed hard.

"Ivar... are you...?" she gasped.

"Beth, get out of here," he ordered. "Run!"

"Stop trying to be all alpha on me," she countered, still gasping for breath. "I'm saving your ass."

"Gerard," Montague yelled. The elder pushed up from the alleyway. "It is good to see you, man. Help me. The prince has come to force you all back to Qurilixen to stand trial. Help me stop him."

Ivar faced Gerard. Was the man in on this?

"No," Gerard stated. "Prince Ivar is an honorable man. Things are not like you said they were. You lied to us. You sent us through the portal believing the royals wanted to control the commoners by withholding our chance at happiness."

Montague yelled. He pulled out a knife. Slashing wildly, he aimed for the nearest target—Beth. She cried out and grabbed her shoulder. The smell of blood filled Ivar's nostrils, and he acted on pure, protective instinct. He leaped and grabbed Montague by the wrist. Montague pushed forward at the same time. Ivar drew the blade hand down, twisting the elder's arm so hard the bone snapped beneath his hand and the blade embedded itself into Montague's chest.

Ivar glanced around in shock at what had happened. He saw a shadow at the end of the passageway start to run toward them. With a groan, he shoved Montague's body into the portal.

"You have to get out of here. People heard the fight and are coming to check it out." Galen appeared with the painting and Beth's bag. "I brought this in case you changed your mind."

"Help me push Hackett through," Ivar said. Gerard helped him lift the unconscious man, and then they hefted his body toward the wall.

"Ivar, go." Beth pushed at his arm, shoving him through before he could speak. The purple light surrounded him, and a loud roar filled his ears like a waterfall was crushing him against rocks. He barely had time to brace himself for the pain as the stabbing sensation of portal travel struck his entire body at once.

Ivar came out of the portal and landed with a hard thud on his back. He scrambled to his feet. The black cave walls were lit with torch light. The tunnels leading to the Draig palace were caved in and blocked. He swung around. Tavas and Montague's bodies were on the ground. Tavas had bled out at the neck, and Montague's knife was still embedded in his chest. Hackett moaned and tried to crawl away on his hands and knees. The dragon-shifter slid on the jagged rocks littering the cave floor and knocked himself on the jaw.

Ivar started to reach for the man when something flew out of the portal and struck his back from behind. He turned, disorientated and ready to fight. It was only the painting Beth had done of him. Another object flew from the portal, and he caught it on instinct. It was Beth's travel bag.

The muffled sound of a scream caught his attention. He glanced towards the cave opening and found Finn, Rafe, and a woman tied up. Their mouths were gagged. Near them, a couple guards were also bound.

Ivar dropped the bag and reached forward as yet another object came out of the portal. This time Beth flew into his chest. He caught her and held her tight. Her camera bag was over her arm, and it bumped into him. "Beth, are you all right? What happened?"

"Oh, damn that stings," she exclaimed. "No one mentioned how much portal travel hurt."

Beth pushed at his chest, and Ivar let her go. Blood marred her sleeve from where Montague had cut her. She grabbed her injured arm. Her eyes moved to the carvings of the dragons and cats that pointed away from the portal as if warning them to turn around instead of going through. She then turned to the men on the floor. Hackett moved too slowly to be an immediate threat.

"Where are we?" she asked.

Ivar rushed to his brother's side and sliced his claw through the ropes to untie him. He pulled the gag out of Rafe's mouth. "Rafe, what's happening?"

"You found Montague." Rafe pulled his brother close, hugging him. "He's behind the rebellions. He must have known where your portal was. These two men pretended to be guards. They jumped us from behind and tied us up. We think they wanted to kidnap you."

"Montague must have arranged this with them before we exiled him to Earth," Finn said, as he gently untied his wife's hands. Ivar recognized the woman they'd called Sadie. "He was supposed to be on an icy tundra. The only way he could've found you was with help."

"So, ah, sorry to interrupt your reunion, but what's he doing?" Beth asked.

Ivar went to her as Rafe and Finn freed the others.

Beth pointed at one of the statues. "I can't read what it says, but is that a bomb or something?"

Hackett had moved close to the statue base. He had reached behind it. Ivar moved to see what Beth was looking at. A timer counted down in the Draig language but the technology looked to be alien to their planet.

"Run," Ivar yelled. He swooped his hand around Beth's waist, lifting her off the ground and running with her from the cave. Finn tugged at his wife's hand. Rafe had untied the guards, and they all leaped from the cave opening to the valley beyond. Beth let go of a small scream as Ivar shifted and pushed faster.

Suddenly a large explosion sounded behind them, and heat blasted at his back. He stumbled and barely managed to keep his footing. He set Beth on the ground, and she fell over. Her body landed in the softer grasses of the valley. Orange light lit her face. He turned to see the danger of the cave. Rocks flew through the air, and a giant rumble sounded from above the mountain. Boulders dropped to bury the cave entrance.

"Run," Rafe ordered.

Ivar reached for Beth's hand and together they ran farther into the valley. He pulled her behind him with his faster speed. When the noise started to subside, they stopped and turned to see the damage that had been done. There was no sign of a cave opening.

"What was that?" Beth asked, stunned as she gasped for breath. She fell to her knees and held her sides.

"Let me be the first to welcome you to Qurilix-en," Sadie said. "I promise, it's not always like this."

17

"I GUESS I know how to make an entrance," Beth said, as they looked at the black stone covering what had once been a cave. They had found safety in a sprawling valley. It was so strange to realize that in one second she had jumped from Oxford, Mississippi into a field of yellow grass. The green sky could not be mistaken for Earth, nor could the three suns over-head. They were just as it had been described—two yellow and one blue. The air smelled sweet, almost too sweet, like spun sugar from the fair grounds. The air felt normal though as it blew against her skin.

Excitement filled her. When she looked at Ivar, she did not feel afraid. She knew she had made the right decision. This is where she belonged.

Aside from the bad guy who had blown up the

cave, no one had been seriously harmed in the explosion. Princes Finn and Rafe led the others to look at the damage. Beth stayed on the ground, looking up at Ivar. "Does this happen here a lot?"

Ivar dropped to his knees and cupped her face. "I don't understand. Did someone push you through the portal? I'm sorry, I don't think..." He turned to the cave-in. "I can't send you back."

"You better not try to send me back. Not after I jumped in that torture tunnel. Portal travel freaking hurts." Beth covered his hands with hers. "You left too soon."

"You pushed me in," he countered. "I didn't want to rush away from you."

"Well, you needed to go before the locals saw you and tried to follow you here." Beth turned her face and kissed his palm. "And I need to tell you something important."

"What?"

"I love you, too, husband." Beth grinned. "Or is it mate? How does this work exactly?"

"I will be anything you want me to be," Ivar said. "I thought you didn't want to come. What changed your mind?"

"You did. Before you just stated I was your woman. You said you regretted us being together. I didn't think you could care for me the way that I was coming to care for you." Beth turned and kissed his other hand. "But then you told me you loved me. And I saw the truth of it in your eyes. That's all I needed. I love you, too. This is where I belong."

He pulled her into his arms and kissed her deeply. Beth closed her eyes. She knew that everything was going to be all right. She felt it as sure as she felt the breath in her lungs and the heart pounding in her chest.

"What do we have here?" Finn teased.

Beth recognized the man she'd met on the streets looking for a bride. Ivar let her go. She stood, brushing off her clothes the best she could. The wound on her arm stung at the movement, and she flinched. Ivar leaned over to examine it.

"It's not too deep," Beth said. "It just stings. I'll be all right."

"Sadie, come here, you remember Ivar, don't you?" Finn motioned to the woman with him.

"Sure, he's the guy who threw me into your arms," Sadie said. "I think you owe him a debt of gratitude."

"I would apologize, but it looks like the gods have spoken," Ivar said.

"Loud and clear," Sadie answered. She touched

her husband's face. "I owe you a big thanks for sending me through to this one."

"This is my Beth," Ivar said. "She saved my life in many ways."

"She saved all of us by seeing that bomb," Sadie said. "Thank you. We're lucky there was no one else allowed in those tunnels today."

"Beth, do you remember Finn from Earth?" Ivar asked. "I believe he tried to marry you."

"Uh," Beth looked apologetically at Sadie.

Sadie laughed. "It's all right. Lover boy here told me all about his Earth adventures."

"I do remember you," Finn said. "I thought you said your ring was being cleaned, and you were already married."

Beth gave him a guilty smile. "I might have lied to spare your feelings."

"And my brother Rafe," Ivar continued the introductions.

"It is very nice to meet you, Rafe." Beth moved closer to Ivar, wanting him near.

"Rafe, this is my wife, Beth." Ivar pulled her to his side.

"I suspected as much by the way you were acting, brother," Rafe teased. "Welcome to the family, Beth. On behalf of all of us, we are pleased to have you join us. My wife will be beyond ecstatic to have another Earth female at the palace."

"Palace?" Beth repeated. "We are going to live in a palace?"

"Of course," Rafe answered for his brother. "That is where princesses live."

"I'm sorry about your portal," Beth said. "Ivar told me how hard you have all been working to keep it open. I know how important it was."

"Yeah, me too." Sadie looked at the rock pile. "I hope they're able to salvage it. I don't like the thought of never returning to Earth for a visit."

"It is most unfortunate," Finn said. "We had only recently convinced the elders to leave it open on a trial basis. Things were looking up for portal travel. One of the last pieces of the puzzle was Ivar's coming home."

"We saw the defected dragons," Ivar said. "They are safe and happy. I had brought proof of their survival with me, but..." He gestured at the cave-in. "I am afraid the evidence is now lost."

"Your word on the matter will have to be enough," Rafe said.

"How bad is the rock slide?" Ivar asked. "Maybe we can undo the damage.

"It doesn't look good," Rafe said. "Montague's

men caved in the palace tunnel before they left for Earth. And it appears like this explosion finished the job. We will have to start over with the excavation. Only this time I don't know if anything can be recovered. It is possible that the blast destroyed the portal forever."

"You know how the people are. Half of them will see this as the will of the gods and won't want to unbury it." Finn scratched the back of his head and sighed in frustration. "We were so close."

"Now my brother is home perhaps we can discuss the offer from that new corporation," Rafe suggested.

"What was it called again?" Finn frowned. "Alien kidnapping bridal service delivery?"

"They call themselves Galaxy Alien Mail Order Brides," Rafe corrected. "I'm telling you. It might be the future of bride procurement."

Ivar shook his head. "If the people did not go for portal travel, I doubt they will agree to a service that brings women to them pre-chosen."

"The gods are not going to love that," Finn drawled. "And I know my people won't. The Draig want little to do with alien visitors. I can't see them ever going for a plan like that, not in a thousand years. They will probably hate the idea more than portal travel."

"It's an option," Rafe said. "And we don't have many left."

"We should begin the journey back to the palace." Finn motioned that they all should start walking. The guards saw their movement, and a couple of them came to join the royals while two stayed next to the rocks. "You know our parents are panicking."

"I am thrilled that you're safe Ivar." Rafe fell into step next to his brother. "So much as happened this last year. There's so much to tell you, and there's undoubtedly so much for you to tell us. Our parents are at the Draig Palace. However, I am sure that the moment the palace tunnel caved in they started their journey here. You can imagine our mother's anxiety about your disappearance. She burned up all her fuel inside the council hall of the elders at the Draig palace."

"She did what?" Beth whispered to Ivar.

"Exploded," Sadie said. "Almost deep fried me. Queen Lassairfhina, your new mom, is an alien called a Feenik. Think something like a phoenix. They explode into a ball of fire and burn off all of their weight when they get overly emotional." Sadie gave a small laugh. "I'm seriously jealous of that diet. When I get emotional, I only gain weight."

Ivar held Beth's hand in his and slowed his steps, so the others walked ahead of them. He smiled down at her. "Where were we before they interrupted us?"

"You mean the part when we were making out?" Beth laughed. She really, *really* wanted to be kissing him right now. "I don't think this is the right time and place for that."

"I meant the part where you said you loved me." He pulled her next to him, so she was against his side as they walked. "And I love you."

"We found this among the rocks," a guard said, joining them. He held up Beth's painting. The frame was broken, and the canvas singed.

"That's beautiful," Sadie said. She looked at Beth. "Did you do that?"

Beth nodded. "I'm a painter."

"The most talented painter I have ever seen," Ivar bragged.

"Wait until you see the collections at the palaces." Sadie grinned. "There is a piece from Earth brought here by my sister-in-law that I think you're going to flip over."

18

EPILOGUE

"You heard the prince. Move a quarter of the way back!" Finn ordered. The soldiers instantly obeyed, running down the rectangular field. They were in the courtyard clearing beside the Var palace.

"Quarterback," Ivar clarified in frustration. "Finn, I said quarterback, not move a quarter of the way back. These Earth words are not translating correctly."

Beth shared a look with her sister-by-marriage, Jenna. The woman had been a bookkeeper in Kansas City before she met Rafe. Well, *met* was putting it mildly. He had shifted, scared the crap out of her, and she'd dinged her head on a lamppost trying to get away. Rafe and Finn had panicked, and when she woke up, she was on Qurilixen.

"Should we help them?" Jenna asked.

"Don't you dare," Eve ordered. Her husband, the oldest dragon-shifter prince, Kyran stood next to Ivar, shaking his head and giving contradicting orders in a failed effort to help explain the rules he didn't quite understand. "This comedy of errors is better than real football."

Beth loved her new castle home. The large building was so stark against the green-blue sky. The red walls of the palace were constructed of locally made brick and appeared like something straight out of an epic fantasy movie. Square towers made up the four corners with narrow chimneys alongside them. Gray smoke came from the tops, creating four cloud-like lines in the sky. Banners featuring a big gold cat on a purple backdrop hung down the towers' sides, and sky bridges connected the tops of them with long open walkways. Beth loved walking across them. The air was so crisp at fourteen stories high.

Several balconies wrapped the main structure, one on each of the second to fifth stories. They were cut into the building rather than sticking out. White gauze covered sections of them to shade them from the sunlight. Shadows moved behind the gauze as people walked past.

"Get 'em, Fire Breathers. Go, team!" Sadie yelled

as she rejoined them, drawing Beth's attention back to the game. Sadie handed Eve a bowl of small fruit for the group to share and then sat down next to them on the blanket.

"You can do it, Furry Claws!" Jenna yelled, her voice a little softer than the others. The women laughed at her, and she shrugged. "I forgot what we're called."

"The Fuzzy Wuzzies Kitten Heads," Eve said.

"We're the Fierce Tiger Claws," Beth corrected, before yelling, "You got this Tigers!"

It was a beautiful day out, and the Draig royal family had joined them at the Var palace. Officially, it was to discuss the idea of an alien bridal delivery service, but that meeting wasn't for a couple of days. Digging out the portal turned out to be complicated. The entire cave system had collapsed, and basically, a mountain sat on top of the portal. It was unknown what condition they'd find it in if they could even find it under all that rock. Either way, the project would take years, perhaps decades to complete.

Beth eyed Ivar's back. He waved his hands in the air as he tried to explain, yet again, the finer points of football to his men. She never thought she would love someone so much. Having jumped into the portal after him was the best decision she had ever made—her leap of faith.

"Oh, you have to finish telling Beth about our husbands' first trip to Earth," Jenna said, laughing as she had obviously already heard the story.

Eve nodded. "OK, so I was working as a kickass rock singer living the nightlife when our four boys show up at one of my shows. Apparently, it was their first time on Earth looking to pick up women. And mind you they had done the research beforehand, so they were really confident in their decisions. Kyran sauntered up to me all decked out like some 1950's version of the urban cowboy—you know, those guys who act country but have never seen a cow. He told me he was a cowman, not a boy."

"Oh, no," Beth covered her mouth, laughing as she looked at Kyran. He appeared so dignified in his royal tunic shirt.

"Sadie, you would have been proud. Finn was dressed up like a great warrior," Eve continued, "also known as a ninja. I kid you not he was head to toe covered in black, mask and all, and look like he was getting ready to rob the place." She lifted her hands and made chopping motions with her arms. "He even did the moves."

Beth laughed harder, falling over to lean on

Jenna. Ivar turned at the sound and grinned at her.

"I'll have to ask him to show those moves to me later," Sadie said, dabbing at her eyes as she laughed so hard that she teared up.

"Then there was Rafe. Jenna, your man was wearing white bell bottoms with a matching long-sleeved sailor shirt."

"*Rawr*," Jenna answered making a clawing gesture toward her husband's back. "Anchors aweigh, matey." When she dropped her hand, she said, "It's better than the time he lost the bet to Rafe. My first trip back to Earth was with my new husband dressed as a pretty ballerina in a tutu. He danced for me in the streets. It was horrifyingly funny."

"What about Ivar?" Beth asked.

"Pretty much what he has on now," Eve said, gesturing at Ivar.

He wore a vest and tight pants with cross lacing up the sides of his legs and under his arms. The tight pants dipped so low on his hip she could see his flat stomach and hip bone. Beth couldn't help it as her eyes roamed over his muscles.

"Oh, that's no fun," Jenna teased.

"But wait, there's more," Eve said. "The best part was when people asked, Ivar told them he was a *draqueen*."

Beth laughed so hard she snorted.

Ivar threw up his hands in frustration and moved to join them on the blanket. He knelt before her and leaned over to place a kiss on her nose. "What is so amusing?"

"Nothing much," Beth said, grinning.

"Eve was telling us about how you and your brothers pick up women," Sadie said.

"Yeah, nothing much, *drag queen*," Eve drawled.

"It's pronounced *draqueen*," Ivar corrected. "And it means royalty."

"Whatever you say, my love." Beth kissed him.

"I'm happy to hear it," Ivar said, his eyes lighting up. "Because I have been telling the princes about cheerleaders, and I think—"

"*Nooo*," the women denied in unison before he could even finish the thought.

"Not a chance." Beth patted her husband on the cheek.

"Can't blame a man for trying." He resumed kissing her, not caring who watched. When he pulled away, he whispered, "I love you, Beth."

"Always," she answered, "and forever."

The End

GALAXY ALIEN MAIL ORDER BRIDES SERIES

Spark

Flame

Blaze

Ice

Frost

Snow

Spark

Mining ash on a remote planet where temperatures reach hellish degrees doesn't leave Kal (aka Spark) much room for dating. Lucky for this hard-working man, a new corporation Galaxy Alien Mail Order

Brides is ready to help him find the girl of his dreams. Does it really matter that he lied on his application and really isn't looking for long term, but rather some fast action? Earth women better watch out. Things are about to heat up.

Flame

Vin (aka Flame) can't believe he's in yet another holding cell. Stupid Earthlings wouldn't know fun if it bit them in the hind quarters. Speaking of fun, the hot little number who claims she's a guard at the jail has been making his body respond in ways he's very happy about. If only she'd get on board with the plan and help him escape back to his ship. First she'd have to believe he's an alien. Right now she's taken to thinking he's crazy.

Blaze

Sev (aka Blaze) isn't looking for commitment, but there is no way in hell he's letting his brother go to

Earth to search for a woman by himself. He's prepared to yank the idiot out of every jail house and ice cream parlor (don't ask) if he has to. It wouldn't be the first time. He can handle a good fight. But what this alpha isn't prepared for was the hardheaded beauty determined to follow him home.

ABOUT MICHELLE M. PILLOW

New York Times & *USA TODAY*
Bestselling Author

Michelle loves to travel and try new things, whether it's a paranormal investigation of an old Vaudeville Theatre or climbing Mayan temples in Belize. She believes life is an adventure fueled by copious amounts of coffee.

Newly relocated to the American South, Michelle is involved in various film and documentary projects with her talented director husband. She is mom to a fantastic artist. And she's managed by a dog and cat who make sure she's meeting her deadlines.

For the most part she can be found wearing pajama pants and working in her office. There may or may not be dancing. It's all part of the creative process.

Come say hello! Michelle loves talking with readers on social media!

www.MichellePillow.com

facebook.com/AuthorMichellePillow

twitter.com/michellepillow

instagram.com/michellempillow

bookbub.com/authors/michelle-m-pillow

goodreads.com/Michelle_Pillow

amazon.com/author/michellepillow

youtube.com/michellepillow

pinterest.com/michellepillow

COMPLIMENTARY EXCERPTS

SPACE LORDS: HIS FROST MAIDEN

A FREE EXTENDED SNEAK PEEK!

by Michelle M. Pillow

Empath and space pirate, Evan Cormier is obsessed with decoding an ominous premonition about his future. When a fellow crewman angered a spirit, the vengeful Zhang An took her wrath out on everyone in the vicinity. Evan just happened to be one of them. He's now facing a future in which he'll be forever alone.

Lady Josselyn of the House of Craven has been betrayed. With her home world on a Florencian moon under attack and her family dead, she finds herself at the mercy of the one who deceived them. There is only one thing left to do—die with honor. But before she can join her family in the afterlife, she must first avenge all that she held dear. Falling in love with a pirate was never in the plan. Evan and his thieving crewmates might have delayed her fate, but they can't stop destiny.

His Frost Maiden Excerpt

Craven Estates, Earth Settlement, Florencia's Fifth Moon

"Lift her," the General ordered, his shiny boots walking away from her, taking her reflection with it.

Two men hauled her to her feet, holding her up by her arms. Josselyn suppressed a cry as they jerked her dislocated shoulder. She couldn't see their faces, didn't need to. Her body hurt so badly she couldn't tell where the pain was coming from anymore.

The one who'd betrayed them stood before her. General Jack Stephans. He'd deceived her family and the fifth moon settlement. He'd traded them in for money and power. Josselyn lifted her gaze briefly to the hard depths of the steel green eyes before her. She wanted to kick, to give one last good blow, to go down fighting, but she couldn't raise her limbs.

"Poor little Josselyn, so heartbreaking," the

General grabbed her chin and swiped beneath her eye. He looked young, was in fact very young for his position, only a few years older than her six and twenty. And yet they all knew so much more of fighting than anyone their age should, than anyone ever should.

"We gave you a home," she whispered. "How could you do this? How could you join them?"

"You gave me a place in your stables," he spat, his grip tightening on her chin, bruisingly so. "Not a place at your table. Not a place by your side. Not equal. They gave me a rank, a title. They give me respect. They give me a place in this world."

"Jack," she said, her voice softening for the orphan boy they'd found over twenty years ago. If she begged him, maybe fate could be turned around; maybe this day could be erased. Fate had spit them out in a whirlwind of chance and deceit. Maybe all that had happened wasn't his fault. Maybe it wasn't hers. None of it mattered. None of it changed the fact that he had taken everything she held dear, everyone, and now he was robbing her of her family home. Her tone hardened and she closed her eyes. "General."

"Look at me, Josselyn," he said. His tone caught even as his grip on her face tightened until his fingers pressed the inside of her cheeks against her teeth. "You're so cold. Even now, your face is composed. Is one, lonely tear all the passion you can muster?"

"I am Lady Josselyn of the House of Craven." Her eyes opened slowly, focusing on the shiny white of his uniform. It gleamed with the orange glow coming from the fireplace. The material looked odd in the drabber earth tones many on the fifth moon wore. Theirs was a world based on Medieval Earth. Each moon in the Florencian system was different, each settlement patterned off a singular time in the human past, times that history had almost forgotten. But the principals of the ancestors who'd established the colonies no longer applied. Times were different now. What had started as preservation of history had turned into reality, into laws and a way of life they all believed in as generation after generation was raised into the worlds of the Florencian moons.

The General shook her by the face until finally she forced her eyes to meet his. He looked angry, hurt, wildly hopeful. "I can save you. I can say you had nothing to do with the treachery of your family. No one wants to kill a woman of noble blood. The line of Craven doesn't have to die. I will take your name; the name denied me by your father."

Was he serious? She knew he'd asked her father

for her hand in marriage. In fact, she'd dismissed the proposal with the full knowledge he only asked because he wanted power. Did he think she could love him now? Want him? Take him into her bed?

He must have read the answer on her face because his own expression hardened. She knew Jack. He wouldn't ask again.

"I suppose not," he said, almost sad. "Even if you agreed, I could never trust you not to take a blade to my back. Not after today." He sighed heavily. "Not after this."

"Ago," she whispered, even her voice beginning to fail in its strength, "pugna quod int-"

"Quiet your tongue! This house is mine. Mine." He let go of her chin and her head drooped. "And you can die knowing that I have taken more than what you all refused to give me in life."

"A place at our table," Josselyn said, her tone softer still, the will to live leaving her. Her heart called out to her ancestors, to her dead family, begging them to come and get her.

"My table," he answered, stepping away. The General lifted a gun, pointing it at her head. She heard the telltale click of metal on metal. The weapon was not one found on the fifth moon. They fought with swords and axes, like the old medieval ways. Though technology was available, not using it was a point of honor. He must have brought the weapon from another moon. Perhaps the Victorians? The Elizabethans? It appeared to be too old to be from much later in time.

"Do it, Jack." She didn't look at him as she waited for the final discharge of the gun, the loud bang before the end. When it didn't come, she repeated, the words a mere mouthing of her lips, "Do it."

"Speed you to a quick end, Josselyn Craven," Jack whispered. "You all brought this on yourselves."

To find out more about Michelle's books
visit www.MichellePillow.com

Space Lords Series

His Frost Maiden
His Fire Maiden
His Metal Maiden
His Earth Maiden
His Woodland Maiden

TAKING KARRE

BY MICHELLE M. PILLOW

Divinity Warriors Book Four
Alternate Reality Romance

Sir Vidar of Spearhead is too busy guarding the borderlands to bother with the headache of selecting a bride. Ordered to marry by the king, he plans to grab a woman and get back to the warfront, never to think of it again. That is until he meets the alluring Lady Karre with her teasing eyes, lush lips and irresistible ways.

Known by many names, inter-dimensional thief Karre, has only one purpose—take down the company that ruined her life. When her luck runs out and she's caught, Divinity Corporation condemns her to matrimony on a primitive, warrior-filled plane where Karre soon discovers there are worse fates than being prisoner to a man with insatiable appetites.

Before long, days and nights filled with bliss becomes something neither expected, and when Karre is taken, Vidar is forced to confront emotions a battle-hardened warrior never expected to feel.

Taking Karre Prologue Excerpt

Three weeks ago, Dimensional Plane 395, Adult Pleasure Centre VWH
Because right now, in this moment, she was their fantasy.

Karre marched out on stage in red stiletto heels, a slinky dress, big grin and nothing else. She kept tempo with the hard, drumming beat of music. Men hollered, whooping their excitement just to see her. She smiled at them, looking over the crowd of heads. She could make them do anything—beg, buy, steal, kill—because right now, in this moment, she was their fantasy.

Blonde hair piled high on her head, garnished with a string of diamonds and rubies some suitor had given her. It was a sweet trinket, one she might even keep, not that she would remember where the jewels came from. She traveled too much and had more important things on her mind.

Karre turned slowly with her arms raised above her head. The hem of her short dress lifted to just below the curve of her ass. When her back was to the crowd, she bent forward. The cheering grew as the men got a peek of the naked treasure hidden beneath the clinging silver. What did she care if they saw her ass? Her pussy? Her breasts? They were just skin, flesh, a tool like any other. No matter how much they wanted her, they would never be able to touch her.

On this dimensional plane of existence, humans cohabitated with humanoid creatures. The first time Karre saw a vampire sucking on the neck of a shifted werewolf, she'd nearly sprinted out of the room to find her wrist portal to flash out of there to another plane. The portable device looked like a large bracelet to most, but to Karre it was her sole means of survival.

Necessity made her stay where she was. This plane was the easiest to get jewels on without resorting to thievery and the hard, shiny rocks were good for trade in nearly every dimension. Besides, not counting the dancing, being in Dimensional Plane 395 was like taking a vacation. With so many strange and different creatures, they never questioned anything she said and most were focused more on blood-drinking and pleasure-seeking.

Being in a new dimensional plane was like being in your world, but only if had it evolved in a different way. To a point, there were many similarities. Languages, generally, were relatively similar, though for some reason the written word consisted of unfamiliar symbols. Some people looked the same, but were not the same people. Natural disasters and major human events were shared. Weather was the same and each place was still Earth.

"I adore you, Sparkle!" a man yelled. "Marry me!"

Karre turned to look over her shoulder at the crowd and winked. A plethora of large green horns, red flesh, reptile skin, webbed fingers, sharp fangs, and ridged flesh stretched out before her until the mass became a single entity flowing back and forth like a wave.

"I'll take that as a yes," the same voice answered her playful flirting. A rush of similar proposals followed the first, showering her in declarations of love. But she wasn't fool enough to believe them. What they felt wasn't love. It was lust.

Karre knew their adoration for what it was and

used it to fuel her dance. She twirled and wiggled, thrust her ass toward them, drew her hips in seductive circles, only to pause in a sexy pose in time with the music. Slowly, she undressed, peeling the slinky gown off her body. Several lights flashed, illuminating her from various angles, leaving no curve unseen.

Just flesh. Just a means. Just another job. Just another plane and soon a distant memory.

Her smile widened, as she knew this was her last dance, at least for this trip. The cheering rose, but she stopped listening. And then it was over. Karre held still, letting the dying notes find their silence before walking naked from the stage.

"You were wonderful tonight, Sparkle," a new dancer fawned. "The crowd loves you. I was wondering if you'd show me how to—"

"Is he here?" Karre asked, stopping the woman from starting a conversation Karre didn't have time for. It's not like she could tell the truth—that all her dancing skill was someone else's memories uploaded into her brain by a device she'd bartered for on another plane.

"He's in your room," the woman answered, frowning slightly at having her question dismissed.

"And he brought a large case. I think it's full of gifts so you'll consider his suit."

"Perfect," Karre grinned. Taking a long robe the woman held out, she slipped it over her shoulders. "I don't want to be disturbed."

Two weeks ago, Dimensional Plane 154, Stac Lesh Mansion
Because right now, in this moment, she was the help.

Karre stared at her red, curly hair in the liquid-silver reflection wall. It had been pulled into a bun at the nape of her neck. The long skirt of the plain uniform and padded body suit did much to hide her figure under the thick gray wool. An apron, changed every time so much as a spot marred the pristine white, covered high over her chest and low to her knees. With the clothes and makeup to pale her face into an unimpressive mask, no one would look twice in her direction because right now, in this moment, she was the help.

She had expected to keep her head down and do her job for months before coming back into this room. But in putting on the uniform, she became invisible. The rich people she worked for didn't look in her direction twice. Well, that wasn't necessarily true. When the wife was gone, the husband had looked at her more than twice. A big grin showcasing blacked-out teeth and a very inappropriately timed belch had changed his interest quickly.

Karre reached to touch her reflection. Behind her, the rich baby's room spread out like the entrance to a palace. Gilded ceilings etched with clouds, golden rays of light and ridiculously cheerful fat angels stretched above as white marble stretched below. It was cold and unwelcoming and more than any one person deserved.

"Oh, wonderful, finally, help," the rich wife said, sweeping into the room. Karre didn't bother to learn the lady's name. "Rich wife" was much easier to remember. The woman held her child under the arms, away from her chest, as if contact with the baby would somehow ruin her carefully planned outfit. "Which one are you?"

"Brigitte, ma'am."

"Take Cinny," the woman ordered. "Mommy needs time to collect herself."

Karre suppressed her groan of frustration at being interrupted and stood to dutifully take the child. She cradled the poor creature close and walked it toward the crib.

"Sing to Cinny before you put her down," rich wife ordered, standing before the liquid silver as she brushed at her clothes.

Karre stopped walking. Sing? To the gurgling, wiggling mass in her arms?

"Well, Brigitte?"

"Mistress, mistress, let me come in," Karre sang the only childlike-sounding song she could think of at the moment, pausing to clear her throat. "I have the pence if you have a quim."

"What a pretty tune," the woman said. "I've never heard it. What does it mean?"

"My dad sang it to my mom," Karre answered, letting the memories she had uploaded into her mind take over her personality—Brigitte of the Fallen Women, a whore's daughter raised in a brothel, adept at blending into new environments. She left off the word "once" before adding the lie, "I'm not sure what it means."

"Carry on."

"Mistress, mistress, I'm stiff as a pin. I need your..." Karre continued, lowering her voice as the woman left her alone with the gurgling, oblivious child. Stopping, she laid the baby down and said,

"Sorry, kid, it's the only song I knew the words to. But I guess it's all right. I turned out just fine with lots of jewels and pretty things and you're too little to understand what any of it means. You should be more worried about growing up in this place with that mom of yours. Now, if you just be good," she paused and tucked a blanket around the infant's body, "I've got a job to do."

Going back to the wall, Karre again reached for her reflection. She stepped forward, letting the liquid hit her hand. It stung, freezing cold in the warm room. For a moment, she hesitated, glancing back at the gurgling child. She thought about grabbing Cinny and taking the baby with her.

"Sorry, kid," she whispered, "even with that mother, you're better off here."

It was a delicate balance—keeping her purpose in her mind while living out the personality and quirks of another—almost like having two people in her head. Karre's hand met with the wall as she felt around, searching for the device she'd hidden. When her fingers met with a smooth, flat surface, she frowned. Putting a second hand to the wall she became frantic, sliding her palms in wide, searching arcs. Perhaps the adhesive she used had come loose. She bent her knees, crouching as she searched the bottom corner of the liquid reflecting wall. Her fingers were so cold it became hard to feel, but the molecular structure of the liquid kept the silver from trickling down her arms as it remained bonded to itself.

Then, to her great surprise, warmth gripped her. A hand wrapped her wrist and jerked her forward. She was pulled through the wall, feeling the sting of silver before landing on a hard, stone floor. Gasping and shivering, she looked around the secret room. A wall of computing towers lined one side, next to three technicians silently typing away on their holographic keypads.

"Lose something, Brigitte?" a man asked, coming close.

Karre glanced up from the floor, "No, sir. I have nothing to lose."

"You are extraordinary." The man laughed. Her eyes instantly took in the familiar insignia of the Divinity Corporation. "Finally, we meet."

Karre forced a grin she didn't feel, letting him see her blackened teeth. Knowing what she looked like, she couldn't help but wonder at his choice of words. Extraordinary? "I wasn't aware we were destined to meet, sir. How lucky for me."

"I can assure you when I'm done with you, you

won't feel lucky." The man leaned down, studying her face. He had the militant rigidity of a soldier, from the purposeful jerks of his body to the engraved frown lines around his mouth and eyes. His hard gaze bored into her, filling her with cold dread. She, or rather Brigitte, had seen that look in men's eyes before. They were usually the kind to beat a prostitute the second they couldn't get their pricks hard.

"I've heard that one before," she mumbled, pretending to be unimpressed.

"I'm Director Tomes and..." He paused, lifting the small, wrist-wrapping device she'd been searching the liquid-silver wall for. Divinity had the only known source of top-secret inter-dimensional travel technology and they wouldn't like the fact that someone had stolen it. "I have a feeling you know where I am from. It was very naughty of you to borrow our only portable jump prototype. Our scientists will be very interested in seeing how you got it to work. This device will make traveling to uncharted worlds much easier. No more carting around temporary portals. No more perfectly timed pickups from headquarters. No more rescue parties."

Less supervision so you can do more dark deeds, Karre silently added.

"We'll be able to explore planes at a much faster rate," Tomes continued, as if it was a good thing.

Just like an infectious disease.

"Sorry, I'm not available for science lessons, but if you'd like to make an appointment, I'm sure I can fit you in," Karre hummed in pretend thought, "uh, never."

"Oh, you're going to be fun to break, my dear," Tomes promised. "Talbert. Get her ready to go."

For a complete, up-to-date booklist, visit www. MichellePillow.com

THE SAVAGE KING

BY MICHELLE M. PILLOW

Want more Var?

Lords of the Var® Series

Bestselling Cat-shifter Romance Series

Cat-shifting King Kirill knows he must do his duty by his people. When his father unexpectedly dies, it's his destiny to take the throne and all of the responsibility that entails. What he hadn't prepared for is the troublesome prisoner that's now his to deal with.

Undercover Agent Ulyssa is no man's captive. Trapped in a primitive forest awaiting pickup, she's going to make the best out of a bad situation...which doesn't include falling for the seductions of a king.

The Savage King Excerpt

Kirill watched the door to his bedroom open. He'd been sitting in the dark, trying to relieve the stress headache that had built behind his eyes for the last week. The pain started at the base of his skull and radiated up to his temples until he could hardly see straight.

A heavy responsibility had been thrust on his shoulders, a responsibility he really hadn't prepared himself for, the welfare of the Var people. King Attor had not left him in a good position. He'd rallied the people to the brink of war, convinced them that the Draig were their enemy, and even went so far as to attack the Draig royal family.

Kirill wanted to see peace in the land. However, he knew the facts didn't bode well for it. The Draig had a long list of grievances against King Attor and the Var kingdom.

Before his death, the king had ordered an attack on the four Draig princes, all of which ended horribly for the Var. The worst was when Prince Yusef was stabbed in the back, a most cowardly embarrassment for the Var guard who did it. If he hadn't been executed in the Draig prisons, he would've been ostracized from the Var community. Luckily, Prince Yusef survived or they'd already be at battle.

Attor had also arranged for the kidnapping of Yusef's new bride. The Draig Princess Olena had been rescued, or that too would've led to war. The old king had even tried to poison Princess Morrigan, the future Draig queen, on two separate occasions. She too lived. And those were only a few of the offenses Kirill knew about in the few weeks before King Attor's death. He could just imagine what he didn't know.

Kirill sighed, feeling very tired. He'd known since birth that the day would come when he'd be expected to step up and lead the Var as their new king. He just hadn't expected it to be for another hundred or so years. His father had been a hard man, whom he'd foolishly believed was invincible.

"Here kitty, kitty, kitty." His lovely houseguest's whisper drew his complete attention from his heavy thoughts.

Ulyssa bent over like she expected him to answer to the insulting call. He dropped his fingers from his temple into his lap, and a quizzical smile came to his lips. As he watched her, he wasn't sure if he was angered or amused by her words.

"Are you in here, you little furball?" she said, a little louder.

She wore his clothes. Never had the outfit looked sexier. His jaw tightened in masculine interest, as he unabashedly looked her over. All too well did he remember the softness of her body against his and the gentle, offering pleasure of her sweet lips. She'd made soft whimpering noises when he'd touched her, yielding, purring sounds in the back of her throat. Even with the aid of nef, he was surprised by how easily and confidently she melted into him. The Var were wild, passionate people and were drawn to the same qualities in others. He suspected she'd be an untamed lover.

Too bad she'd belonged to his father first. In his mind, that made her completely untouchable though none would dare question his claim if he were to take her to his bed. Technically, by Var law, she belonged to him until he chose to release her. For an insane moment, he thought about keeping her as a lover. He knew he wouldn't, but the thought was entertaining.

Kirill's grin deepened. Ulyssa strode across his home to the bathroom door with an irritated scowl. It was obvious she didn't see him in the darkened corner, watching her. He detected her engaging smell from across the room, the smell of a woman's desire. It stirred his blood, making his limbs heavy with arousal. And, for the first time since his father's death, his headache relieved itself.

"Hum, maybe I'm looking too high. I'm sure there has to be a little cat door here somewhere. Come here, little kitty. Where are you hiding?"

His slight smile fell at her words. It was easy to detect her mocking tone.

"Where's your little kitty door, huh?" Ulyssa whispered to herself, her blue gaze searching around in the dark.

Kirill grimaced in further displeasure. He watched her open the door to his weapons cabinet. Her eyes rounded, and he thought she might take one. She didn't. Instead, she nodded in appreciation before closing the door and continuing her search for an exit.

She stopped at a narrow window by his kitchen doorway. Her neck craned to the side, as she tried to see out over the distance. Kirill knew she looked at the forest. From under her breath, he heard her vehement whisper, "Where exactly did you little fur balls bring me? Ugh, I need to get out of this flea trap, even if I have to fight every one of you cowardly felines to do it. I've fought species twice as big and three times as frightening. A couple of little kitty cats don't scare me."

If this insolent woman wanted to play tough, oh, he'd play. Curling gracefully forward, Kirill shifted before his hands even touched the ground. He let one thick paw land silently on the floor, followed by a second. Short black fur rippled over his tanned flesh, blending him into the shadows. His clothes fell from his body, and he lowered his head as he crept forward. A low sound of warning started in the back of his throat. He was livid.

**To find out more about Michelle's books
visit www.MichellePillow.com**

PLEASE LEAVE A REVIEW

THANK YOU FOR READING!

Please take a moment to share your thoughts by reviewing this book.

Be sure to check out Michelle's other titles at www.MichellePillow.com